The Divine Arbiter and Other Stories

Munshi Premchand

Translated by Dinesh Verma

Printed by CreateSpace, an Amazon.com Company

Digital version of this book is also available on Kindle and other devices on Kindle and other retail outlets.

Copyright © 2017 Dinesh Verma
All rights reserved.
ISBN: 9781522025665

Acknowledgements

I am grateful to Google.com and Time-Life photograph archives for the photograph used on the cover page, which depicts an unknown Indian Village towards the first half of the twentieth century.

I am also grateful to Canva.com for allowing the use of its excellent user-friendly software resources for designing the cover page of this book.

Table of Contents

1. Introduction — 1

2. Brief Biography of Munshi Premchand — 7

3. The Chess Players (*Shatranj Ke Khiladi*) — 11

2. The Inspector of Salt (*Namak Ka Daroga*) — 30

3. The Elder Brother (*Badey Bhaisaheb*) — 46

4. The Divine Arbiter (*Panch Parmeshwar*) — 61

5. The Shroud (*Kaffan*) — 83

6. Mother (*Ma*) — 97

7. A Goddess (*Devi*) — 126

8. A Winter Night (*Pous Ki Ek Rat*) — 153

9. The Thakur's Well (*Thakur Ka Kuan*) — 164

10. Captain Sahib (*Kaptan Sahib*) — 170

11. Glossary — 185

The Divine Arbiter and Other Stories

Introduction

Munshi Premchand is one of the most celebrated writers of the Indian sub-continent and a pioneer of Hindi fiction.

Premchand lived and wrote when India was a colony of the British. At that time almost 90% of India's population lived in villages and its rate of illiteracy too was almost as high. Agriculture was the main occupation of was a vast majority of the population which in turn was dependent entirely on rains and vagaries of nature. The Indian society was still beleaguered by centuries old evils like a feudal system with rampant exploitation of farmers by landlords and that of poor landless by the farmers; untouchability; complete subjugation of women in the society with its manifestations in child marriage, dowry system and strong a taboo against widow remarriage.

Premchand's writings belong to the tradition of realist fiction. According to him literature is a critique of the human existence: "*sahitya jeevan ki alochna hai*". Most of his works therefore are a faithful reflection of the harsh social realities of his time. Though most of his novels and stories are set in the present day Uttar Pradesh, the social phenomena that find its reflection in his work prevailed all over the country; for, irrespective of the region, language or the drivers of the economy, the social relations and the plight of the common people and women in particular were more or less similar all over the country.

In spite of his firm belief in an author being a faithful recorder of the social realities, Premchand did not consider literature as a means for social transformation. He was not a propagandist, theorist or even a social reformer. He is in essence a story teller whose primary raw material was human beings. What interested him was the character, mental dilemmas and actions of human beings. The stories included in this collection explore vividly the personality of the characters involved and their mental conflicts. Premchand has thus created an extensively wide spectrum of characters ranging from feudal lords, noblemen, government officials, prosperous farmers to landless labourers. Many of these characters have become archetypical characters in Hindi fiction.

During his life time Premchand wrote more than a dozen novels and about two hundred fifty stories. Included in this collection are of some of the most famous stories written by Premchand. They cover on a microcosmic level almost all the themes dealt by Premchand in his entire *ouvre*. They also contain a fair sample of his style of writing and his language and idiom, which is a fine amalgam of Urdu and Hindi. However it is not to suggest that anyone interested in his writings should remain content after reading these stories. The real genius of Premchand is to be found only in his novels especially 'The Gift of a Cow' (*Godan*) and 'The Embezzlement' (*Gaban*).

All the stories included in this collection have unique themes and characters. 'The Chess Players', the first story in this collection is entirely different from the others as it is set in Lucknow of 1856 in the background of deposition of Wazid Ali Shah, the *nawab* of Avadh by the British Army. It explores the theme of moral decadence in a society that has become totally immersed in pursuit of pleasures.

Dharma, which is an all encompassing Hindi expression for various English words like values, moral obligation and principles, is an important and recurring theme in Premchand's works. The moral conflict arising from the need to adhere to one's *dharma* is the central theme in 'The Divine Arbiter', 'The Inspector of Salt' and also to some extent in 'The Goddess'. The protagonists in these stories are confronted with an intense moral dilemma and they have to make a choice between what their *dharma* dictates and an alternative. In 'The Divine Arbiter' the alternative available to the protagonist is spoiling one's relationship with one's lifelong friend and in 'The Inspector of Salt', it is closing one's eyes and allowing a big consignment of salt to be smuggled away and in the process ingratiating oneself with a fat bribe. In 'The Goddess' the dilemma is even more intense as here the protagonist, a young low caste woman is confronted with the choice of saving, at great peril to her own personal safety, the honour of the widow of a high caste man who was once infatuated with her and who committed suicide after she had shamed him for making a sexual advance towards her. Out of respect for the true love that the spurned lover bore towards her, Tuliya has to decide whether to put at stake her own *dharma* to safeguard that of the wife of the dead lover.

To someone living in the twenty first century in which the newspapers carry some account or the other everyday of human choices and actions which seem to be reaching a new low with each passing day, the dilemmas like those referred to above may not appear to be very intense. That however only shows how far we have come from the days in which these stories are set and the transformation that has taken place in our value systems.

Even though he wrote in a period which now appears to be a distant past with a value system that seems now to be on verge of extinction, Premchand's works include a number of themes that came into vogue much later and have great importance even today at least in Indian society.

One such theme is the position of woman in the society. Premchand's works are replete with narratives of sad plight of tradition bound women in villages and small town of India as manifested in dowry system, child marriage and taboos on widow remarriage. Although these practices may appear to be relics of some distant past, these customs still survive in the some parts of India. Another important theme that appears to be rather futuristic in Premchand's works is the modern feminist woman who is an activist and an entrepreneur who bears all the burdens of the family on her shoulders. Among the stories included in this collection, this aspect of womankind is brought out to some extent in 'Mother'.

The plight of the marginalized landless farmers and the downtrodden is the dominant theme of 'The Shroud', 'A Winter Night' and 'The Thakur's Well'.

Relationship between siblings is yet another interesting subject dealt with in 'The Elder Brother'. Along with this primary theme of relationship with one's elder brother the story also explores a subsidiary them: the impact of the English education system introduced during the colonial period on the mental makeup of young students.

Written in an inimitable but simple language of day to day use, these stories provide an excellent introduction to the corpus of Premchand as well as a peep into the Indian society during the late nineteenth and early twentieth century. Replete with satire, irony and incidental humour which is typical to the writing of Premchand, these stories also provide a delightful reading.

The Divine Arbiter and Other Stories

Brief Biography of Munshi Premchand

Munshi Premchand, whose original name was Dhanpat Rai was born on 31.7.1880 in a small village near Benares. He was the fourth son of his father who worked as clerk in a post office. His childhood and early life were mostly troubled and unhappy. His mother died when he was eight. His father remarried and his stepmother was not too affectionate towards him. In 1997 his father too passed away. In 1995, two years before his death, his father got Premchand married, when he was merely fifteen years old, to a girl from a comparatively richer family, who was not only not good looking but had a quarrelsome nature. Thus after the death of his father the responsibility of supporting a family of five including his step mother, wife and two brothers fell on the shoulders of Premchand.

Premchand joined a *madarsa* in a neighbouring village when he was seven years old where he was taught Urdu and Persian by the local *maulvi*. In 1890 he got himself enrolled at Queen's College in Benares. To support himself and his family after the death of his father, he started giving tuition to the child of an advocate for five rupees a month. In 1900 he got the job of an assistant teacher at Government District School Baharaich. He had never been at very good terms with his wife due perhaps to her bad temper. She finally left him and started living with her parents. In 1906 Premchand married a widow in spite of considerable opposition that he had to face, as widow re-marriage was not considered as acceptable in the conservative Indian society at that time. It was only after his second marriage that things started looking up a little for Premchand.

Premchand developed an interest in Urdu literature quite early in his life. During his younger days he even took up a part time job with a book seller which allowed him access to lots of books, which he could not have done on his own expense. He started writing when he was just 13 years old. In 1905 Premchand got posted to Kanpur where he met Daya

Narain Nigam the editor of magazine *Zamana* in which he published a number of his articles and stories.

To begin with he started writing by his nick name Nawab Rai. In 1905 his first story 'Duniya Ka Sabse Anmol Ratan' or 'The Most Precious Jewel of the World' was published in *Zamana*. In 1907 he published a short novel *Hamkhurma-o-Hamsavab* which was later published as 'Prema' in Hindi, which dealt with the issue of widow remarriage in Indian society.

In 1907 Premchand's first collection of five stories by the name *Soz-e-Vatan* was also published. These stories dealt primarily with the sad plight of the people in the country. The publication of this collection was seen as critical of the colonial administration and it led to the search of the real author who wrote these stories. In 1909 when Premchand was working a Deputy sub-Inspector of Schools, he was raided and 500 copies of *Soz-e-Watan* found with him were burnt. Premchand was released but asked to give an undertaking not to write without prior permission. It was to circumvent this interdiction that he adopted the pseudonym Premchand. The first name Munshi is an honorary prefix which was added by his fans as a sign of respect for him.

Premchand started writing in Hindi from 1914. In 1919 he translated some of his own works from Urdu to Hindi like *Seva Sadan* which was originally *Bazaar-e-Husn*. He was promoted as Deputy Inspector of schools in 1921 after completing his BA from Allahabad in 1919. He resigned from the government job in 1921 after which he went back to Benares to concentrate on his literary career. He suffered considerable financial difficulties and ill health. He was however successful in establishing his own printing press in 1923 some of his own books like *Rangabhumi*, *Nirmala*, *Pratigya* and *Gaban* were printed.

Premchand also had a short dalliance with the Indian film Industry. In 1934 he got a job of a script writer at Ajanta Cinetone Production House at Bombay. He wrote the script of 'Mazdoor' (The Labourer), a film by Mohan Bhawnanai, in which he also performed a cameo of leader of a labourers' union. However Premchand did not find the environment of the Bombay film industry to be quite conducive to his nature and he returned to Benares after his one year contract expired.

In 1936 he contracted some illness and after suffering for some time he died in October 1936 at an age of 56.

In his personal life Premchand remained a very simple and down to earth person who remained miles away from exhibitionism or self aggrandizement of any kind. Premchand wrote about a dozen novels and 250 short stories. Among the most famous of his novels are *Godan* (*The Gift of a Cow*) and *Gaban* (*The Embezzlement*).

The Chess Players

It was the time of Wazid Ali Shah. Lucknow wallowed in the pursuit of pleasure. Big or small, rich or poor, everyone was sunk in the morass of self-indulgence. Some found their enjoyment in dancing and singing sessions; others managed to derive it merely in a dose of opium. In every sphere of life it was the pursuit of pleasure that manifested itself. Whether it was administration; literary or social circles; art, commerce or industry; it was this streak of hedonism that manifested itself everywhere. The state officials indulged themselves in sensual enjoyment, poets in narration of love and pains of separation; artisans in *kalabattu*[1] and *chikan*[2] embroidery and traders were busy selling collyrium, perfumery and cosmetics.

The intoxicating effect of this pleasure seeking could be seen reflecting itself in everyone's eyes. No one was concerned with what was happening in the rest of the world. Here one could see a partridge fight in progress. Elsewhere the preparations for a quail fight would be in progress. Or it would be *chausar*[3] that would be laid out amidst the din of on-lookers. At yet another place it would be an intense battle of chess that would be razing. From king to the most ordinary person everyone seemed to be humming the same tune.

This infatuation for pleasure had reached such a level that even beggars, after they had received their alms, would look for opium or some intoxicant rather than buy bread. 'Playing chess, *ganjifa*[4] or cards sharpens your mind, improves the thinking power and you get habituated to solving complicated matters.' These kinds of arguments would be advanced by many with great passion.

So if Mirza Sajjad Ali and Mir Roshan Ali too spent most of their time in sharpening their minds in this manner, what objection could be there to any rational and thinking person? Both owned large estates and had no worries about earning a livelihood. They would spend the entire day sitting and chatting at home. What else could they do after all? Every morning after breakfast, both the friends would settle down with a chessboard in front of them, arrange the pieces and then the moves and counter moves would commence. Thereafter, they would not be concerned whether it was afternoon or evening or the day was over. Again and again messages would be sent from inside that their food was ready. A reply would be sent that they would be there soon; let the table be set. In the end the cook would be constrained to lay down the food in the drawing room itself and the friends would perform both the tasks simultaneously.

Mirza Sajjad Ali did not have any elder at home; therefore, the sessions would take place in his drawing room. It was not as if others in his household were happy with his conduct. What to talk about the family members, the neighbours and even the domestic servants commented with disdain every day:

'It is an accursed game. It destroys the family...god forbid if someone gets addicted to it...it makes you a good for nothing person...it's a disease.'

Even Begum Sahiba, the wife of Mirza was so averse to it that she would always look out for an opportunity to reprimand him. However she found hardly any occasion for it. She slept till late in the mornings; in the meanwhile the chessboard would already be set. At night she would be asleep by the time Mirza would return to her bedchamber. She would of course keep venting out her anger on the domestics.

'They are asking for *paans*[5]? Tell him to come and collect it himself...They have no time for eating? Go and throw the food on their table...they may eat it if they want or let the dogs feed on it if they so desire.'

However she could not say anything to him in person. In fact she was not so upset with her husband as with Mir Sahib. She had named him Mir Bigadu[5]. It was perhaps because Mirza *ji*[6] would ascribe all the blame to Mir Sahib while giving his explanations.

One day Begum Sahiba had a headache. She told her maid, 'Go call Mirza Sahib. Let him bring some medicine from the doctor. Go, hurry up.'

When the maid went and told him, Mirza said, 'I will be there soon.' Begum Sahiba was in a foul mood. How could she tolerate that the husband keeps playing chess while she is suffering from headache? Her face turned red. She said to the maid, 'Go and tell him that he must come immediately otherwise I would go to the doctor on my own'. At that time Mirza *ji* was at a very exciting juncture in the game: another two or three moves and it could be the mate for Mir Sahib. Feeling irritated he said, 'Is she on her last breath? Can't have even a little bit of patience!'

Mir said, 'Why not go and hear what she wants to say. Women are always a little temperamental.'

Mirza: 'Yes and why should I not go! After all, it is a matter of two moves or so and it is going to be the mate for you.'

Mir: 'Don't be under such illusions. I have thought of such a move that your pieces will remain where they are and it would be mate for *you*. Go and listen to what she is saying. Why hurt her feelings unnecessarily?'

Mirza: 'Now that you say that, I'll go only after it is mate for you.'

Mir: 'I will not play. You go and hear what she has to say.'

Mirza: 'What *yaar*[7], I will be obliged to take her to some doctor. I know she doesn't have any headache; it is just an excuse to irritate me.'

Mir: 'Whatever it is, you have to do that for her sake.'

Mirza: 'All right, let me make one more move.'

Mir: 'Not at all…until you go and listen to her I will not touch the pieces.'

Mirza Sahib felt obliged to go inside. Begum Sahiba changed her stance but said in a pained voice, 'you are so enamoured with this godforsaken chess. I may die but you will not deign to get up. I doubt if there would be any other man like you.'

Mirza: 'What can I say, Mir Sahib refuses to listen. It was with great difficulty that I managed to get rid of him.'

Begum: 'Why, does he think everyone else too is a good for nothing person like him. I'm sure he too has a family and children; or is it that he has got rid of all of them.'

Mirza: 'He is a big chess addict. But as he comes here to visit me I feel obliged to play.'

Begum: 'Why don't you tell him to get lost?'

Mirza: 'He is a man of my own standing; in fact, two notches higher than me in age as well as social stature. Therefore, I have to give him some regard at least for that.'

Begum: 'Then, I will myself tell him to get lost. Let him feel annoyed, if he so desire. It is not as if we are dependent on him for our living. Hariya, go and bring the chess board from the drawing room. Tell Mir Sahib that Mirza Sahib will not play now; that he may leave.'

Mirza: 'No no, don't do such an outrageous thing. You want to bring disgrace upon me? Wait Hariya, where are you going?'

Begum: 'Why don't you let her go? If anyone stops her it would be as if he sucks my blood. All right you stopped her; let me see if you can stop me.'

Saying that the infuriated Begum Sahiba walked towards the drawing room. Poor Mirza's face turned pale with helplessness. He started pleading with his wife, 'For God's sake I implore you in the name of Hazrat Hussain. All right anyone who goes there will see my dead body.'

But Begum did not pay any heed. She went up to the door of the drawing room but suddenly her feet seemed to get tied down at the thought of facing a man who was not her husband. She peeped inside. There seemed to be no one there. Mir Sahib had changed the positions of a few pieces on the board and as if to show his innocence, he was taking a stroll in the veranda outside. Embolden by his absence, Begum went inside, overturned the chess board and threw some of the pieces under the bed and some in the veranda and locked the door from inside. Mir Sahib, standing at the threshold saw the pieces being flung out and heard the sound of glass bangles. When the door was locked from inside, he understood that the Begum was in a foul mood. He thought it best to head to his home.

Mirza said, 'It's really unbelievable what you have done.'

'Now, if ever Mir Sahib comes here I will have him shown the door. If you had shown so much devotion to God as to this chess game you would have become a *wali*[8]. You are forever playing chess and I am wrecking my head over the household affairs. Now are you going to the doctor or not?'

When Mirza left his home, instead of heading towards the doctor, he reached the house of Mirza Sahib and narrated the whole story to him. Mir Sahib said, 'When I saw the pieces falling out of the window, I guessed as much that very moment. So I ran off immediately. She seems to be a woman with a short temper. But the way you have pampered her is also not done. How does it matter to her what you do outside the home. Her duty is to take care of the household; why does she have to meddle with other things?'

Mirza: 'Any way, tell me where we are going to have our sessions now.'

Mir: 'What is there to worry about? I have such a big house. Let's start playing here itself.'

Mirza: 'But how am I going to bring my wife to agree to it? When I was staying right inside the home, she was so upset. Now if I sit here the whole day she will probably not leave me alive.'

Mr: 'Let her keep venting out her anger; in two three days she will be all right. But you must do at least this much: today onwards be a little strict and assertive with her.'

II

For some unknown reason the wife of Mir Sahib considered it apposite that he remained away from home. She never criticized, therefore, his fondness for chess; on the contrary sometimes when Mir Sahib would be late in leaving she would remind him of it. For this reason Mr Sahib had developed an illusion that his wife was of an extremely modest and serious nature. However when the chess sessions started taking place in their own drawing room and Mir Sahib started staying at home the entire day, his wife started feeling very uncomfortable. Her independence was getting affected. She would yearn the entire day for an opportunity to peep out of the door.

The domestics also started gossiping. Till now they had been twiddling their thumbs the entire day. They were not bothered if anyone came or left the house. Now they were under pressure the entire day. Sometime they would be ordered to bring *paan*, sometimes to bring sweetmeats. And now the hookah fire would be smouldering the entire day like the heart of a lover. They would go to the Begum Sahiba and complain to her that Sahib's chess had become a veritable slavery for them and how running around the whole day they had developed boils on their feet.

'What kind of a game is this where you start in the morning and don't let up till the evening! It is enough to play for an hour or two to amuse oneself. But then who are we to complain; we are after all our master's slaves, whatever orders you give we'll have to execute...but this chess is a very inauspicious game. No one who indulges in it has ever prospered; some catastrophe or the other surely befalls the household. Entire neighbourhoods are known to have got ruined because of the addiction of one person. Here in the whole neighbourhood everyone is talking about this only. We are obedient servants of our master. But we feel bad hearing such things talked about him every day. But what can be done?'

Hearing this, Begum Sahiba said, 'As far as I am concerned, I myself don't like it. But if he does not listen to anyone then what can be done.'

In the neighbourhood the few old timers that were still left started speculating about all sort of inauspicious happenings, 'Now there is no saving us. When this is the state of the wealthy people then god only can help the country. The entire kingdom is going to be destroyed due to this chess. Prospects are very bleak indeed.'

In the kingdom anarchy prevailed already. People were robbed in broad day light. There was no one to hear their grievance. The entire wealth of villages around was flowing to Lucknow and getting squandered on prostitutes, performers and various other pursuits of self indulgence. The debt of the English Company[9] was increasing day by day. Due to lack of good governance even the annual taxes were not being collected properly. The Resident[10] issued warnings time and again but everyone here was intoxicated with pursuit of pleasure; no one was bothered in the least.

Anyway, many months had passed since the chess sessions started in the drawing room of Mir Sahib. Every day new gambits were tried, new castles made and new formations were employed. Sometimes there would even be recriminations and it would even come to exchange of hot words but the two friends would make up soon. Sometimes it would so happen that the game would be given up and Mir Sahib would leave the drawing room and go inside his room and Mirza *ji* would return to his home feeling annoyed. But the mental rancour would come to end after an overnight sleep. Next morning both the friends would again assemble in the drawing room of Mir Sahib.

One day both the friends were deeply immersed in their game of chess, when an officer of king's army riding on horseback came enquiring about Mir Sahib. Mir Sahib was scared out of his wits. 'What is this calamity that has befallen on us? What is this summons for? Now there seem to be no saving us from the doom.' All the doors were ordered to be closed. The servants were instructed to inform the trooper that Mir Sahib was not at home.

Trooper: 'If not at home then where is he?'

Servant: 'I don't know about that. But what is the matter?'

Trooper: 'What can I tell you? He is summoned at the court. Perhaps some soldiers are to be requisitioned for the army. Is he a landlord or what! When he has to go to the front he will realize what it is all about.'

Servant: 'All right, you may go. He will be informed.'

Trooper: 'Informing him is not the issue. Tomorrow I will come myself. I have been ordered to bring him along.'

The trooper left. Mir Sahib was petrified. He asked Mirza *ji*, 'Tell me sir, what to do now?'

Mirza: 'It's a big problem indeed. I hope I too have not been summoned.'

Mir: 'The wretch said he will come again tomorrow.'

Mirza: 'It's a misfortune, what else? If we are to go to the front, we might die for nothing.'

Mir: 'There is only one way out; just don't *be* at home when he comes. Tomorrow onwards we can go and install ourselves in some deserted spot across the Gomti River. Who will come to know about it? The fellow will come and go back on his own.'

Mirza: 'Great, what an idea! And there seems to be no solution except for this.'

On the other side, the Begum of Mir Sahib was telling the trooper, 'That was really a smart trick you played on them.'

'I can make such idiots play around my little finger. All of their intellect as well as courage have been devoured by chess. Now onwards they will not stay at home even by mistake.'

III

The next day onwards both the friends started leaving their home while it would still be dark. Holding a small carpet under their armpit, carrying a box full of pan, they would go across the Gomati to an old deserted mosque, which was built perhaps by Nawab Asafudollah [11]. On the way they would pick up tobacco and *chillum*[12] and once they would be at the mosque, they would spread the carpet, prepare the hookah and start with their chess game. Thereafter, they would not be concerned any more with anything in the world. Except for a few words like check or mate, no other phrase would come out from their mouths. Not even a yogi would be so concentrated in his meditation. In the afternoon if they would feel the pangs of hunger they would go and have some food at some wayside *nan*[13] shop and after having a bout of hookah thereafter their battle would recommence. Sometimes, they would not even bother about food.

On the other hand the political situation in the country was becoming terrible day by day. The Company forces were advancing towards Lucknow. There was turmoil in the city. People were fleeing to the villages taking their families along. But the two players were not at all concerned with that. Passing through the lanes and by lanes every morning, they would be scared lest anyone in the employ of the King happened to catch a sight of them and they got apprehended for nothing. They wanted to consume the proceeds of their estates worth thousands of rupees per year without doing anything in return for the King.

One day both the friends were playing chess in the ruins of the mosque. Mirza was on a somewhat weak footing. Mir Sahib was posing him checks again and again. At that moment soldiers of the Company were seen approaching. It was a White Army which was coming to capture Lucknow.

'English army is approaching, god help us.'

Mirza: 'Let them come, first guard yourself against the check, here is the check.'

Mir: 'We should watch them, let's come and stand aside here under a cover.'

Mirza: 'You may watch them after a while, where is the hurry, another check.'

Mir: 'There are canons too. Must be five thousand young men…their faces look like those of red monkeys. Seeing their faces alone one gets a fright.'

Mirza: '*Zanab*[14] don't make excuses, try these tricks with someone else, here is a check.'

Mir: 'You are a strange person. Here there is a calamity over the city and you are thinking only of check. Have you got any idea, how we are going to get back home if the city is surrounded.'

Mirza: 'We'll see when it is time to go home. Here is a check. Now it is the mate.'

The army passed by. It was ten in the morning. The game commenced again.

Mirza: 'How are we going to manage our food today?'

Mir: 'Today it is a day for fasting. Are you feeling very hungry?'

Mirza: 'No, but I wonder what's happening in the city!'

Mir: 'Something or the other must be taking place. People must be sleeping after having their food. *Huzoor* Nawab Sahib must also be in his pleasure chamber.'

Once both the gentlemen started again with their game they went on till three in the afternoon. Now Mir appeared to be the weaker party. It was about four o'clock when the sounds of the retreating army could be heard. Nawab Wazid Ali had been taken into custody and the army was taking them towards some unknown destination. There was neither any furore nor massacre in the city. Not a drop of blood had been shed. Till that day, perhaps no other sovereign of an independent state had been defeated in such a peaceful manner without a drop of blood being shed. It was not *ahinsa*[15] on which the gods bestow their blessings. It was the height of cowardice, on which even the biggest cowards would shed their tears. The ruler of a huge state like Avadh was made a prisoner and its capital, Lucknow slept soundly wallowing in luxurious. This was the lowest ebb of political downfall in the kingdom.

'Huzoor Nawab Sahib has been captured by these tyrants,' said Mirza.

Mir: 'Let it be, here is a check.'

Mirza: '*Zanab*, let's stop a while. In a moment like this you don't feel very nice. Poor Nawab Sahib must be shedding tears of blood at this moment.'

Mir: 'What else he has except to cry. Would he get such luxuries there in custody? Check.'

Mirza: 'No one has good times forever. What a painful situation it must be!'

Mir: Yes that it is indeed; here another check! Now this is the end, there is no way you can be saved.'

Mirza: 'By god…you are so heartless. You don't feel sad even after witnessing such a sad event. Oh poor Wazid Ali Shah!'

Mir: 'First save your king; thereafter you can mourn Nawab Sahib. Here it is a check and here is the mate!'

The army passed by taking the king away as a captive. As soon as it left Mirza set up the board once again. The pangs of defeat are terrible. Let's read a prayer mourning Nawab Sahib' said Mir. But Mirza's patriotism had vanished after his own defeat. He was getting impatient to take his revenge.

IV

It was evening. Bats had started screaming in the ruin. Birds had returned to their nests. The two champions, however, were still continuing with their game. Mirza *ji* had lost three games one after the other; the situation of this fourth round too was not very encouraging. He would start every round with a firm determination to win and play carefully; yet one or the other of his move would turn out to be bad which would ruin his game. With every defeat the feeling of revenge got intensified even further. On the other hand Mir Sahib, who was feeling thrilled as if he had found a hidden treasure, sang *gazals* and cracked jokes. Mirzaji was getting annoyed listening to him but complimented him in order to get rid of the embarrassment caused by his defeat. But as his game became weaker and weaker he was losing patience. He had started getting irritated over every small thing, '*Janab*, please don't change your moves. What is this, you make a move and then you change it. Whatever you have to move do it only once. And why are you keeping your hand on the piece? Leave it alone. Don't touch the piece till the time you have thought over your move. You are taking hours to make a move. This is not done. He who takes more than five minutes to make a move would be considered defeated. Here, you have changed your move again! Please keep the piece back there where it was.'

Mir Sahib's queen was getting eliminated. He said, 'When did I make a move at all?'

Mirza: 'You have already made the move. Now please keep the piece back, at the same place where it was.'

Mir: 'Why at the same place? When did I take away my hand from it?'

Mirza: 'Now if you don't leave the piece till eternity, it is not to be considered as a move? The moment you saw your queen getting eliminated you started playing tricks.'

Mr: 'It is you who play tricks. Victory or defeat is destined; no one can win by playing tricks.'

Mirza: 'So this time it is mate for you.'

Mir: 'Why should it be mate for me?'

Mirza: 'Then leave the piece where it was kept before.'

Mir: 'Why should I keep it there? I won't.'

Mirza: 'Why won't you keep it there? You will have to.'

The arguments started getting intensified. Both of them were adamant when it came to their stand. Neither of them was ready to give up. Conversation started losing the context. Mirza said, 'If someone even in your extended family had played chess, you too would have known its rules. They were engaged in mowing grass; so how could you be expected to play chess. Owning an estate is not the same thing. If you are awarded an estate it does not become you have become a nobleman.'

Mir: 'What? Your own father might have been a hay-trusser. Here in our family people have been playing chess for generations.'

Mirza: 'Go tell that to someone else; they spent all the life working as a cook at Gaziuddin Haidar's place and now you are posing as a noble. Being a noble is not a joke.'

Mir: 'Now why do you want to spoil the name of your forefathers? It must be they who might have been working as cooks. Here, we have been dining on the same table as the King.'

Mirza: 'Oh come on now crazy fellow, don't be such a braggart.'

Mir: 'Mind your tongue or you will regret it. I am not used to hearing such words. If someone dares to challenge me, I'll take out his eyes. You have the guts to dare me?'

Mirza: 'You want to test my guts, so come along. Let's cross our swords and decide it right away.'

Mir: 'Who do you think you are trying to scare?'

Both the friends pulled out their swords. Those were the days of kings and *nawabs*; everyone carried swords and daggers. Though pleasure seekers both of them, they did not lack valour. Political fealty had reached its lowest ebb in their hearts: why fight or lose one's life for the king or the kingdom. However there was no dearth of personal bravery in them. Both of them fell down wounded and lost their lives writhing in agony. They from whose eyes not one tear came out for their King, those very beings had given up their lives defending a queen of chess.

It had become dark. The chess board lay there on the floor. Both the kings, seated on their respective thrones seemed to cry over the death of the two braves. Silence prevailed all around. The ruined arches, the falling walls and the minarets covered with dust watched silently and mourned over the corpses of the players of chess.

The Inspector of Salt

When the new Department of Salt[16] was created and dealing in what was considered a god given substance became illegal overnight, people started trading in it clandestinely. Various types of manipulations and subterfuges came into existence. Whereas some got their work done by paying bribes, others resorted to cunning. For the officers of the Department it was a windfall. Leaving aside even the most respected job of a *patwari,* the record keeper of village lands, everyone seemed to be aspiring for the Department of Salt. Even the advocates felt tempted for the post of an inspector in this department.

It was the time when people considered an English education and the Christian faith to be one and the same thing. It was Persian that dominated in every sphere. After studying love stories and romantic poetry people well versed in Persian could get appointed to highest ranking posts.

Munshi Vanshidhar too, after finishing the account of Zulekha's unrequited love and considering Shirin and Farhad's love story and the battle of Nal and Neel to be something more important than discovery of America, started on his quest for an employment.

His father was an experienced person. He advised, 'Son, you know very well the sad plight of the family. It is weighed down by the burden of debt. The daughters, they are growing up like wild grass. As for me, now I am like an old tree on the edge of a road, which no one knows when it may fall down. You alone are responsible now for the family.'

'When it comes to a job, don't look at a post as it is like the shrine of a *pir*[17]. Your aim should be at the offerings and the *chaddar*[18] covering it. Try to find a job where you earn something over and above your salary. The monthly salary is like the full moon which is sighted only once and then gets smaller every passing day and disappears. The money you receive over and above it that is like a flowing stream which quenches your thirst all the time. Salary is given by employer; there is no appreciation in it. The under the table earnings are a gift of God; prosperity comes from that alone. Now you are yourself a learned person, what more do I have to make you understand.'

'In these matters, discernment is very important. Judge the person, see how desperate he is for getting his work done and look for the opportunity; after that do what is appropriate. It is always profitable to be tough with someone who needs a favour from you. However it is difficult to make him fall in line if he does not need any favour. You must always keep this in mind; this learning is the sole capital that I have amassed over my entire life.'

After that homily, the father gave him his blessings. Vanshidhar was an obedient son. He listened to him with due attention and then set out from home. In the immense world patience alone was his friend; good sense his road map and self dependence his support. But he had set out under an auspicious star: soon after he left he got appointed as an inspector in the Department of Salt. A good salary and as for incidental income there seemed to be no end of it. When the old *munshiji*[19] received this news his heart swelled with happiness. The creditors softened a little; as for the neighbours, they started feeling the pangs of jealousy.

*

It was a cold winter night. The *sepoys* and guards of the Salt Department were feeling nicely intoxicated. It was not over six months since Munshi Vanshidhar had arrived here; yet even in such a short time he had won over his seniors with his exemplary conduct. The officers had started reposing enormous trust on him.

One mile to the east of the Salt Office flowed the Yamuna on which there was a pontoon bridge. The Inspector was sleeping with all the doors closed. All of a sudden he woke up hearing the rumbling of carts and the shouting of boatmen in place of the usual sound of water flowing by. He got up.

'Why are these wagons crossing the river so late in the night? Surely there is something shady going on. His logic supported his suspicion. He wore his uniform, placed his revolver in the pocket and soon enough he reached the bridge riding on his horse. Seeing a long queue of wagons crossing the river, he asked in an angry tone,

'Whose carts are these?'

Silence prevailed for a while. The men whispered among themselves and then the one on the front said, 'They belong of Pandit Alopideen.'

'Who is Pandit Alopideen?'

'The one from Datagunj.'

Munshi Vanshidhar was taken aback. Pandit Alopideen was the most eminent landlord of the region. He dealt in millions of rupees. Was there anyone around whether high or low who was not in his debt. His business too was very spread out. He was a very shrewd operator. The English officers, when they visited his region for hunting used to be treated as his guests. All the year round it would be like a festival at his place.

Munshi asked where the carts were heading to. 'Kanpur,' someone replied. However when asked what was loaded on them there was utter silence. The Inspector Sahib got even more suspicious. After waiting for some time for a reply he said in a loud voice,

'Have all of you become deaf? I am asking you what is loaded on them?'

When he did not receive any answer he took his horse to the side of one of the carts and felt a sack with his hand. His doubt was removed. It contained lumps of salt.

Pandit Alopideen was following half asleep half awake in his decked up carriage. Suddenly some alarmed cart drivers came and woke him up and said, 'The Inspector has stopped the carts and he standing near the bridge and calling for you.'

Pandit Alopideen had unshaken faith in money power. He used to say that what to talk about this world, even in heaven it is money that reigns supreme. What he said is the reality indeed. Justice and principles are often like toys in the hands of wealth which makes them dance to its tunes. He kept lying on the berth and said proudly, 'Carry on we are coming.' Having said that, he made a few *pans* quite nonchalantly and put them in his mouth. Then covering himself with a blanket he came to the Inspector and said, 'Greetings *babuji*[20]! What such crime has been committed by us that the wagons have been stopped. At least we Brahmins should have the favour of your kind blessings.'

'The government's orders', said Vanshidhar in a dry manner.

Pandit Alopideen laughed and said, 'we don't know the government's order or the government. For us you are the government. Between you and us it is like a family affair; can we ever be something apart from you? Your good self took the trouble unnecessarily. It cannot be that we pass this bridge and don't make our offerings to the god of this riverbank. I was preparing to come personally to be at your service.'

Vanshidhar was not impressed at all by that sweet talk of lucre. It was newly born upsurge of honesty.

'We are not one of those traitors who go around selling their soul for a few pennies. You are under arrest at this moment' he said in a stern voice, 'You will have to abide by the rules. That's all; I don't have time for any further talks. Constable Badlu Singh. I order you take this man in custody.'

Pandit Alopideen was transfixed. There was commotion among the cart drivers. It was perhaps the first occasion in the life of Panditji that he had to hear such harsh words. Badlu Singh advanced but he was too overawed to dare to hold his hand. Panditji had never witnessed principles showing such disrespect to riches. He thought that the man was stubborn that he had not yet got into the money trap. He is inexperienced and hesitant. He said in a very humble voice, '*Babuji* don't do that, I will be ruined. My reputation will be reduced to dirt. What will you gain by humiliating me? Are we different in any respect from your own?'

'We don't want to hear such things' said Vanshidhar firmly.

The support that Alopideen was taking to a rock seemed to be slipping under his feet. His self respect received a severe jolt. However he still had complete confidence in the might of money. He said to his secretary, '*Lalaji* present notes of one thousand rupees to Babu Sahib; his good-self is becoming like a starved lion.'

Vanshidhar got angry and said 'One thousand or even one hundred thousand can not detract from the right path.'

Alopideen's was feeling quite exasperated by this mindless obstinacy and rare godlike renunciation. Now a battle started between the two powers. Wealth pounced and leapt and made its attack. From one to five, five to ten, ten to fifteen and from fifteen it reached twenty thousand, but the Principles held their ground with immense fortitude and stood unshaken like a mountain in front of the immense army.

Alopideen lost hope and said, 'I cannot dare to go beyond that. Now you have the right to do what you want.'

Vanshidhar prodded the constable. Badlu Singh advanced towards Alopideen cursing the Inspector in his heart. Panditji got startled and withdrew a few steps. He said with immense humility, 'Babu Sahib, have mercy on me, I am ready to settle for twenty five thousand.'

'It is impossible.'

'Thirty thousand.'

'Not possible at all by any means.'

'Not even for fourty thousand?'

'Fourty thousand...it is not possible even for fourty lac. Badlu Singh arrest this man. Now I don't want to hear even one more word.'

The principles trampled the lure of wealth under their feet. Alopideen saw a strong and burly man carrying handcuffs approaching him. He looked around with hopelessness and apprehension and then fell down unconscious.

*

The world slept but its tongue was awake. By morning from the child to aged everyone was speaking of the same thing. Everyone was commenting on the conduct of Pandiji; criticism and taunts were showering from all sides, as if the sin of the sinner had been eradicated from the world.

The milkman who sells water in the name of milk, officers who fill in fictitious log books, officials who travel without train ticket, rich men who make forged documents, all of them were wagging their tongues as if they were gods.

The next day, as accused Pandit Alopideen proceeded towards the court, wearing handcuffs, with his heart full of self contempt and disappointment and his neck bent downwards with shame, there was uproar in the city. People's eyes would perhaps not be so anxious even in a carnival or a fair. All the rooftops as well as boundary walls were crowded with onlookers.

However it was to be only till he reached the court. Alopideen was the lion of that impenetrable forest. Most of the officers of the court were like his acolytes, court clerks like his servants, advocates executors of his command and as for peons, orderlies and guards, they were like his unpaid slaves.

The moment they saw him coming people came running from all the corners. Everyone was amazed: not because Alopideen had done such a deed but how he could he fall into the dragnet of law? How could a person owning so much wealth with which he can find all the means and who is such a smooth operator could get into the trap of law. Everyone seemed to show sympathy towards him.

With great alacrity a battery of reputed lawyers was deployed. The battle of principles and wealth commenced, this time in the courtyard of justice. Vanshidhar was standing silently. He had no strength except for truth, no arms except for plain speaking. There were witnesses but greed had rendered all of them unreliable.

It had come to a pass when Vanshidhar felt that even justice seemed to be a little withdrawn from him. It was a court of law but its functionaries were all overcome by favouritism. How can favouritism and justice be friends to each other? Where there is preferential treatment how justice can even be imagined to be given. The suit came to a quick end.

The Deputy Magistrate wrote in the order that the evidences produced against Pandit Alopideen were unsubstantiated and imaginary. He is a man of great substance. It is beyond even the realm of imagination that he would do something so reckless for small gain. Although the Inspector of Salt Munshi Vanshidhar is not much to be blamed, it is regrettable that his obstinacy and thoughtlessness led a gentleman to suffer so much of discomfiture. We are glad that he is so alert and active in his duty; however, his overzealousness towards the Salt regulations seems to have corrupted his good sense and power of discrimination. He should be careful about it in future.

The advocates heard the judgment and jumped with joy. Alopideen walked out smiling. His close associates were showered with money. His generosity knew no bounds: its waves shook the very foundation of the court building.

When Vanshidhar stepped out he was showered with arrows of sarcasm. The peons and orderlies bowed and saluted. However, at that moment each and every unsavoury word and gesture added to the burning fire of his self dignity and pride. He would perhaps not have walked out with such a swagger had he been successful in the suit. Today he had a strange and distressing experience of this world. Justice, learning, high sounding designations, big beards, flowing cloaks—none of them seemed to be worthy of true respect.

Vanshidhar had taken animosity with wealth. He had to pay its price. Hardly a week had passed when he received a letter of termination. He got punished for devotion to his duty. The poor fellow started back for his home with a heavy heart feeling sorry for himself.

The old *munshiji* had already been whining that even though he had given such sound advice to this lad before he left he did not care two hoots about it. 'He does everything in his own way. Here I keep listening to the reminders from the grocer and the butcher; keep sitting around like a beggar in this old age and there he gets nothing but a bare salary! I have also been in service and I did not have such a designation. But I worked, worked wholeheartedly but then he is out to show his honesty! Let there be total darkness in the house but you must go and light a lamp in the mosque! I pity such intelligence. It is so sad; all his studies and learning have gone waste absolutely.'

After a few days when *Munshi* Vanshidhar reached home in such a sorry state and his old father heard the news he struck his palm on his head with despair. 'I feel like breaking your head as well as my own!' he said. He kept regretting over what had happened for a long time. He even said some harsh words and if Vanshidhar had not gone away from there, his anger would have got transformed into an even uglier form. The old mother also felt very sad. Her desires for a pilgrimage to Jaggannath and Rameshwaram were reduced to naught. As for his wife, she did not even deign to talk to him for many days.'

A week passed in this manner. It was an evening. The old munshiji was sitting and turning the beads of his rosary invoking the name of god Rama when a richly decorated carriage came and stopped in front of the door. It had green and pink curtains and drawn by a pair of bullocks with blue strings around their necks and their horns gilded with copper. A number of servants wielding long sticks on their shoulders were accompanying it.

Munshiji ran out to welcome and saw that it was Pandit Alopideen. He made an elaborate bow and started off with flattering words, 'It is a great honour indeed that your feet have touched our door step. You are like a god to us. But what face do we have to show you, covered as it is with blackening. But what to do, my son is an unfortunate wretch; otherwise how could it be that we would think of hiding our face from your good self. It is better if God keeps one childless instead of having such a progeny'.

Alopideen said, 'No brother, don't say that.'

Munshiji said with surprise, 'What else do I say for such an offspring?'

Alopideen replied in an indulgent voice, 'Pride of family and one who brings glory to the name of his ancestors! How many such upright persons are there, who would sacrifice everything for the sake of their principles?'

Pandit Alopideen said to Vanshidhar, 'Inspector sahib, don't consider it as flattery. There was no need for me to take so much trouble to come here to flatter you. That night you had got me arrested by virtue of your official power; today, however, I come to your custody of my own accord. I have seen thousands of rich and wealthy persons, I have dealt with thousands of persons holding high positions, however if there was any one who overpowered me that was you. I made everyone else a slave of mine and of my wealth. Please allow me to make a submission to you.'

When he had noticed Alopideen Vanshidhar had got up to welcome him but maintaining his self dignity. He thought that Alopideen had come to humiliate him and make him feel sorry. He did not make any attempt at apologising; on the contrary he had found the words of his father to be quite unbearable. However, when he heard what Panditji had to say the misgivings in his mind were wiped out.

Vanshidhar gave a fleeting glance towards Pandiji's visage; it seemed to reflect good faith. Pride now bowed its head before modesty. Feeling a bit shy he said,

'It is your magnanimity that you say that. Whatever discourtesy has taken place on my part, kindly excuse that. I was fettered by the chains of my principles; otherwise, I am your humble slave. It would be my pleasure to carry out whatever order you give.'

'That day at the bank of the river you had not acceded to my request; however today you would have to do so.' said Alopideen in a very respectful manner.

'I am not sure what am I competent for; however, whatever service I could render, there would be nothing lacking in that' said Vanshidhar.

Alopideen took out a letter of appointment made on a stamp paper and placing it in front of Vanshidhar he said, 'Accept this post and sign it. I am a *Brahmin*, I will not leave your door till you accept this request of mine.'

After Munshi Vanshidhar finished reading that letter, his eyes started flowing with gratitude. Pandit Alopideen had appointed him as the manager of his entire estate. Apart from a salary of six thousand rupees per annum, he would be entitled to daily allowance, a horse for transporting himself, a bungalow to live in apart from servants and attendants. He said in a trembling voice, 'Panditji, I am not competent enough to praise you for your magnanimity; but I don't think I am eligible enough for such a high post.'

Alopideen laughed and said, 'right now it is none but an eligible person that I require.'

Vanshidhar replied in a serious tone, 'I am your humble servant. It would be my good fortune to serve a renowned and a gentlemanly person like you. But I neither have qualifications or good sense nor the temperament that could make up for these shortcomings. You need an experienced and astute person for such a job.'

Alopideen took out a pen and said, handing it over to Vanshidhar, 'I am looking neither for learning or experience nor for astuteness or competence. I have had enough experience of the worth of these skills. Now my good fortune and opportunity has given me that pearl in front of which the lustre of qualifications and learning get faded. Take this pen and do not think much about it, just sign it. I only pray to the almighty that you always remain that discourteous, obstinate, stern but principled Inspector that you were at the river bank that day.

Vanshidhar's eyes were flowing with tears. The narrow receptacle of his heart could not contain such a favour. He looked once again towards Pandiji with devotion and reverence and with a trembling hand put his signature on the employment letter.

Filled with joy Alopideen embraced him.

The Elder Brother

My brother was five years elder to me but three years my senior. He too had started studying at the same age as I had; however in a matter as important as education he did not like to be too much in a hurry. He wanted to lay a strong foundation on which a magnificent edifice could be built. He would complete a work that could be done in one year in two years. Sometimes it could take even three years. After all, if the foundation was not sound, how the house would be stable.

I was younger, he was my elder. My age was nine years, his fourteen. He had therefore a birth right to look after my welfare and to keep a watch over me. As for me, courtesy demanded that I considered his order to be like an edict.

He was very studious by nature. He would always be found sitting with an open book and perhaps to give some respite to his brain, he would sometimes make sketches of sparrows, dogs or cats in his notebook or in the margin of his book. At times he would write the same name, word or sentence ten or twenty times. Sometimes he would copy a verse again and again very neatly. There were instances when he would make a composition that would have neither meaning nor any consistency; for example, once I noticed the following written on his notebook: special, Amina, brothers-brothers, in fact, brother-brother, Radheyshyam, Mr. Radheyshyam, in an hour, followed by the sketch of a man's face. I made efforts to find some meaning out of that riddle but I did not succeed and I could not dare to ask him. He was in the ninth standard; I in fifth. To be able to understand his composition would be something beyond the competence of a youngster like me.

I could never put my heart into studies. To sit down with a book even for an hour was extremely difficult for me. The moment I found an occasion, I would go out into the field and jump around or fly paper airplanes and if by chance I found some companion than it would be something out of the world. We would climb up and jump from the boundary wall or ride over the iron gate moving it back and forth, deriving the pleasure of riding on a motor car in the process. However the moment I would return to the room I would be scared to death seeing the terrifying face of my brother. His first question would be,

'Where were you?'

Forever the same question asked in the same voice and for me the only answer would be silence. I don't know why the words, 'I was just playing outside' could not come out from my mouth. My silence would convey the admission of my guilt and there would be no alternative for my brother but to welcome me with words full of indignation.

'If you study English in this manner, you will spend your entire life without mastering a word. Learning English is not a game that you could play when you like; if it were so every good for nothing person on the roadside would be an expert in English. You have to strain your eyes day and night: it is only through blood, sweat and tears that you achieve this learning. And what learning, it is merely to say that you have learnt it. Even great scholars cannot write chaste English, leave apart speaking it. And I would dare say what an imbecile you are that you do not derive a lesson from me.

You see with your own eyes how assiduously I toil; if you don't notice that it is nothing but a fault of your eyes or perhaps your intelligence. There are so many fairs and carnivals. Have you ever seen me going for any of them? Every day there is a cricket or a hockey match. I don't venture to go even in their vicinity. I am forever studying and yet I remain in the same standard for two to three years. How do you expect then that you will pass if you are whiling away your time in games and idle pursuits? For me, it takes just two to three years; you would keep rotting in the same standard all your life. If you have to waste your life in this manner, it is better that you go back home and play *gulli-danda* [21] at ease. Why waste the hard earned money of *dada* [22] in this manner?'

I would start shedding tears after such a rebuke. After all there was no excuse. It was I who had committed the fault, who else would face the reprimand? My elder brother excelled at the art of sermonizing. He would speak such piercing words, shoot maxims and adages like arrows that would break my heart and I would feel absolutely discouraged. I could not find in myself that kind of capacity to toil like a galley slave; so in that state of hopelessness I sometimes wondered why should I not just go home. Why should I waste my life doing something that is beyond my capacity?

It was acceptable to me to remain an imbecile but the thought of doing so much labour made me swoon. However after feeling disappointed for a few hours the clouds of frustration would disperse and I would resolve that from then onwards I would work hard putting in the best of my effort. Immediately, I would draw a time table. Without first making a roadmap how could I start the work? In that time table, there would be no space earmarked for any sport. Get up early in the morning and after a wash and breakfast start studying by six o'clock. From six to eight English, eight to nine arithmetic, nine to nine thirty history; thereafter breakfast and then school. At three thirty return from school and then rest for half an hour and thereafter from four to five geography, five to six grammar followed by a stroll for half an hour in the hostel compound, six thirty to seven English composition then after dinner translation from eight to nine, from nine to ten Hindi, ten to eleven miscellaneous subjects and then retire to sleep.

It is one thing to prepare a time-table but to act in accordance with it is entirely different. Lack of compliance with it would begin from the very first day. The soothing verdure of the green fields, the waft of mild breeze the bouncing of football, the tactics of *kabbadi*[23] and the agility of volleyball would unconsciously and compulsorily draw me away and I would forget everything else. I would not remember anymore of that gruelling timetable and all those books and my elder brother would get an occasion to sermonize and humiliate me. I would run away even from his shadow, try my best to remain away from his sight. I would return to the room stepping so softly that he would not even notice me. The moment he looked up and noticed me it would be as if it was going to be my end. I could sense a naked sword hanging over my neck forever. Even then like a man on his death bed, whose mind is still fettered by the bonds of the worldly pleasures, I could not bring myself to give up sports in spite of the rebukes and reprimands of my brother.

II

The annual examination took place. My brother failed and I passed and stood first in my standard. Between him and me, a difference only of two years remained now. I felt like taking my elder brother to task: 'what happened to all that hard labour of yours? Look at me, I kept on playing all the time and yet I have stood first.' However he was so unhappy and disheartened that I genuinely felt sympathetic towards him and the very thought of sprinkling salt over his wounds appeared to be so shameful to me. I certainly felt a little proud of myself and my self esteem also grew and my brother did not have anymore that authority that he had been wielding over me. I started participating freely in sports. My mind was made up now. If he again tried humiliating me I would say, 'what great exploit have you achieved toiling your sweat and blood! As for me, I have stood first even while playing games all the time'. Even though I could not dare to say those words, it was clear from my very bearing that the terrorising sway my brother had had over me did not exist anymore.

My brother could easily make it out; after all he was very perspicacious. One day when I returned just in time for food, after consecrating an entire forenoon to *gulli-danda*, it was as if my brother had drawn a sword from the scabbard and pounced on me,

'I see that after you have passed this year and stood first it has gone to your head. However my dear brother you should know that the vanity of even the mightiest does not last; who are you to talk about. In your history classes you must have read about the sad plight of Ravan. What lesson did you draw from the character of Ravan? Or perhaps you read it just for the sake of it? It is not enough to just clear an examination; the real thing is mental development. You must understand the real meaning of what you read. Ravan was the master of the entire world. They call such a king a *Chakravarti*. These days the size of the British Empire has grown considerably but one cannot call them *Chakravarti*. There are numerous nations who do not accept the suzerainty of the British: they are absolutely independent. Ravan was a *Chakravarti* king. All the kings of the world paid tribute to him. Even the gods were like his slaves. The god of fire and water were his slaves; but how did Ravan meet his end; his vanity led to the obliteration of even his name. There was no one left who could offer him even a few drops of water. A man may indulge in any vice but he should not fall prey to vanity; he should not assume airs. You become vain and that is the end of yours.'

You must have also read about Satan. He thought that there was no one who was more loyal to the God than him. In the end he was thrown out of the heaven. As for you, you have merely passed one standard and it has already gone to your head; it is unlikely that you would advance much. Take it that you have passed not because of your efforts but it was like a blind man catching a bird. But a bird can fall into your hand only once but not again and again. It so happens that sometimes while playing *gulli-danda* one makes a blind shot. But one does not become a great player just by that. A truly accomplished player is one who loses no shot.

Don't think much of my failure. When you reach the next standard you will realise how hard it is to pass: when you will have to struggle with algebra and geometry and read the history of England. It is not easy to remember the names of the kings. There have been eight Henrys. Which incident took place in the time of which Henry; you think it is an easy task? Write Henry the Seventh in place of Henry the Eighth and you will lose all marks. You will not even get a zero, not even a zero! Which world are you living in! There have been dozens of James, dozens of Williams, scores of Charles; all that makes you head spin. These wretches could not even find names; so they kept on adding second, third, fourth and fifth after the same name. Had they asked me I could have suggested thousands of names to them.

And God alone save you from geometry! In place of a b c you write a c b and you lose all your marks. No one asks these merciless examiners, what after all is the difference between a b c and a c b and why they massacre the poor students for it. You have *dal*[24], *roti* and rice or rice, *dal* and *roti*, what difference does it make? But what do they care about it, these examiners? They want to see only that what is written in the books. They want that boys should remember everything letter by letter. And this learning by rote has been termed education. After all what is the use of learning all such things which neither have a head nor tail?

Draw this perpendicular on that line so the base would be twice as long as the perpendicular. Ask them how does it matter? Instead of becoming double let it become four times or let it just remain half, I don't give a damn. But if you have to pass the exam you have to remember all this inanity. It would be said, 'write an essay on punctuality which should not be less than four pages'. Now you curse them with your notebook opened and your pen in your hand. Who does not know that punctuality is a very good thing? It adds discipline in one's life and the others start liking you for that reason and that you start making progress in your business with it; but how to write four pages about such a small thing? Why waste four pages writing about something that can be described in one sentence? I consider it as sheer absurdity. It would not be economizing time but its utter misuse if you squeeze in something for nothing. I would prefer that a man says quickly, whatever he wants to say and then carries on. But no, you will have to fill four pages, write whatever way you do and the pages have to be full length pages. Now if this is not torture of poor students, what else is it? The worst is that it is demanded that one should write briefly. 'Write a brief essay on punctuality which should not be less than four pages!' Right! Since it was brief they ask for four pages, otherwise they might have made you write a hundred pages. Run fast and that too slowly. Isn't that ridiculous? Even a child would understand such a small thing, but these teachers do not have even that much of sense. On top of it they claim that they are teachers. When you come to my standard, my boy, you will have to suffer all this drudgery and then you will realise the worth of what I am telling you. Right now you have stood first so you seem to be in the seventh sphere, but you have to listen to what I tell you. I might have failed but I am elder to you; I have more experience of life than you do. Take a good note of whatever I am telling you otherwise you will regret it later on.'

It was almost the time to go to school; otherwise god alone knew when that homily would have come to an end. That day I found my food to be quite tasteless. When after passing I am subjected to such sarcasm, it is possible that if I were to fail perhaps my life itself may be taken. The dreadful picture that my brother had painted of the studies in his standard had terrified me. Why I did not run away from the school and went home was in itself a surprise; however, in spite of such taunts my indifference to books remained the way it was. I would not let go off any occasion to participate in games. I used to study but very little: just enough to ensure that the daily task was done and I did not face humiliation in the class. The self confidence that I had developed evaporated in thin air and once again I was living like a thief on the sly.

III

Once again the annual examinations took place and it was yet another coincidence that I passed and my brother failed once again. I had not worked very hard but I do not know how I stood first in my class. I was myself amazed by that. My elder brother had worked hard like a galley slave. He had revised every letter of the course working till ten in the night then getting up at four in the morning and working till going to school at nine. His visage had lost its lustre. But the poor fellow failed. I felt pity for him. When the result was declared he cried and I too started crying. My elation at getting passed was reduced to half. Had I failed my brother would not have felt so sorry for me; but then who can avoid the destiny.

The difference between me and my brother had now been reduced to just one standard. A devious sentiment had its origin in my mind: what if my brother fails yet another time and I become his equal. How then he would be able to beleaguer me; however, I drove that mean thought forcefully out of my mind. After all he rebuked me only in my own interest. No doubt I find it unpleasant that time but it is perhaps the result of those very homilies that I am getting passed again and again and that too with such good grades.

This time my brother had mellowed down a little. Many a times even when he found an excuse to chastise me he exercised patience. Perhaps he had himself started realizing that he did not have the right any more to admonish me and that if it still remained than very little of it was left. My independence increased. I started taking unfair advantage of his tolerance. I started feeling that I would pass in any case whether I study or not; that I had an exceptional destiny. Therefore whatever little I used to study due to the fear of my brother also came to a stop. Now I developed a new passion for flying kites and most of my time would now be consecrated to this pursuit. In spite of it I respected my brother and whenever I flew kites it was away from his sight. All the preparations for the kite flying tournament would be done on the sly. I did not want to give my brother any reason to suspect that my respect and regard for him had decreased in any manner.

One evening, far away from the hostel, I was running desperately to catch a kite that flew with its string dangling in the air. My eyes were towards the sky and mind at that traveller in the sky that was swaying slowly as it proceeded towards its downfall. There was a throng of boys carrying poles with thin branches of trees attached to them chasing to catch that kite. No one seemed to be bothered about what was happening around him. It was as if all of them were flowing with that kite in the sky, where everything was on the same plane and there was neither any car nor tram or any other vehicle.

All of a sudden I ran into my brother who was perhaps returning from the market. He caught me by my hand right there and said angrily, 'Don't you feel ashamed running along with all these street urchins for a kite that is not worth a dime? You are not even conscious that now you are not in the lower classes and that you are now in the eighth class and just one standard below me. A person should after all think a little at least about his position. There was a time when those who passed eighth standard used to become junior administrators in districts. I know so many of such middle-passed who are now first class deputy magistrates or superintendents. There are so many of them who passed merely the eighth standard and who are now our leaders and editors of newspapers. They even have highly learned people working as their subordinates; whereas you, even after reaching the eighth standard you are running after a kite along with these hooligans. I feel sorry for your lack of common sense. I know you are intelligent, but of what use such intelligence that does not care a bit for self-dignity?

You must be thinking in your heart that you are merely one standard below your brother and that he does not have the right any more to say anything to you; however you are mistaken if you do so. I am five years elder to you and even if you reach the same standard as I am in—and if the present sort of examiners are to continue then without any doubt you would be there in the same class as me next year or perhaps reach even higher the following year. However you or even god cannot efface this difference of five years that exists between you and me. I am five years elder to you and I will remain so forever. You would not be able to match the experience of life that I possess; even if you finish your M.

Phil, D. Phil. or D. Litt. One does not acquire wisdom by reading books. Our mother has not passed any standard whatsoever and perhaps even our father did not go beyond the fifth. However even if both of us read all the books in the world, our mother and father will always have the prerogative to guide us or to correct us. Not merely because that they gave us birth but because they have more experience of life then we do and that they will have forever. What kind of government or administration is there in USA, how many times Henry the Eighth got married, or how many planets are there in the sky: they may not know much about these kinds of things, but they have more knowledge about thousands of things than you and I have.

God forbid, if I were to fall sick today, you will simply panic. Apart from sending a telegram to *dada* you would not be able to think of anything more. However if *dada* were to be in your place, he would neither panic nor send any telegram to anyone. He would first of all try to understand the malady and try to cure it on his own; if he does not succeed then he will call for some doctor. Any way illness may be a big thing, you and I don't even know how to manage our monthly affairs. Whatever *dada* sends us, we finish that by twentieth or twenty second of each month and after that we are hankering even for pennies. We start skipping breakfast, start avoiding even the sight of the barber and laundry-man. Yet in half the amount that you and I are spending these days, our father spent a very big part of his life living with dignity and having a good name in his setup while raising a family of nine.

Just think of our headmaster sahib. He has an M.A and an M.A not from here, but from Oxford! He earns a thousand rupees, but who manages his household? His old grandmother! The degree earned by headmaster sahib failed here. Earlier, when he used to run his household himself; he was not able to manage. He used to run debts all the time. Ever since his grandmother had taken over the control, it is as if the goddess Luxmi herself has blessed the household. So my dear brother, drive away the thought from your mind that since you have reached near me and you totally independent now. I know that whatever I am saying must be like poison to you.'

I was absolutely swayed by this new tactic of my brother. I really had the experience of my smallness that day and I developed a new respect towards my brother. With eyes full of tears I said, 'No, not at all. Whatever you are saying is true and you have all the right to tell me that.'

Brother Sahib embraced me and said, 'And I don't forbid you from flying kites. Even I feel tempted to do that. But what can I do? If I myself follow the wrong path then how can I protect you from that? After all that responsibility too lies on my head.'

It so happened that at that very time an orphaned kite flew past above our heads. Its string was hanging in the air. A group of urchins was running after it. My elder brother, who was tall jumped in the air and caught the string and then ran heedlessly towards the hostel. I was running behind him.

The Divine Arbiter (Panch Parmeshwar[25])

Between Jumman Shaikh and Algu Chowdhary there was an intimate friendship. Their lands were tilled together. They also shared some business interests. Each had absolute faith on the other. When Jumman had gone for Haj he left his house in the custody of Algu and whenever Algu had to go away somewhere, he would leave his house in the hands of Jumman. They did not have similar eating habits nor did they share any bond of religion; only their thinking matched with each other's. The essence of friendship too is that itself.

The seeds of this friendship were sown when both the friends were young boys and Jummarati, the father of Jumman used to teach both of them together. Algu rendered great service to the *guruji*[26] washing his cups and plates all the time. There would never be an occasion when his *hukkah* would remain idle, for every chillum would give Algu a respite of half an hour from his books.

Algu's father was a man with traditional ideas. He reposed more faith on service rendered to the guru than to studies as such. He would say that education is not attained through studies and that it is only through the blessings of the guru that you acquire true education. All that matter is the grace and kind regard of the *guru*. Therefore if the blessings of Jummarati Sheikh or his constant company did not have the requisite beneficial effect on Algu, then he could find solace in the thought that he had left no stone unturned in acquiring education and if learning was simply not there in his destiny, how he could attain it.

Jummarati Sheikh however did not much believe in blessings. He had more faith in his stick and it was due to the power of his stick that he was well known and worshipped in the neighbouring villages. When it came to a deed or legal draft prepared by him, even the court clerks could not find any fault in them. The postman, constable or the orderly of the local administrator all looked up to him. Therefore if Algu was held in esteem for his wealth, Jumman Sheikh was respected by everyone because of his learning.

Jumman Sheikh had an old aunt. She owned some land but she did not have any close relative. Jumman had got its title transferred to his name by making big promises to her. As long as the gift deed was not registered enormous amount of hospitality was extended to the old aunt. She was fed delicious victuals: *halva* and *pullav* were almost showered on her. However the seal of registration seemed also to put a seal over this hospitality. Now along with food, Jumman's wife started offering the old aunt some harsh and piercing words as accompaniments. Jumman Sheikh also became a little cold towards her. Now the poor aunt had to listen to such words almost every day.

'How long the old woman is going to live. She gave us only two three *bighas*[27] of arid land but it is as if we have become her slaves. She refuses to eat her *rotis* unless some nice *dal* is given to her. With the amount of money that we have consigned to her belly we could buy the village.

The old aunt tolerated it for a few days; however when she could not bear it anymore, she complained to Jumman about it. Jumman did not consider it appropriate to meddle with the household administration. It continued for some more time in that manner. In the end one day the aunt said to Jumman, 'Son it would not be possible for me to carry on living with you. You start giving me some rupees; I will start cooking something or other for myself on my own.'

'Do rupees grow on trees here?' Jumman replied impudently.

'Don't you feel that I need a little bit to survive on' she said very politely.

'We had not thought that you have come here after taking an animosity with death?' replied Jumman in a serious tone.

The aunt lost her temper and threatened to approach the *panchayat*. Jumman laughed, the way a hunter laughs in his heart when he sees a deer approaching the trap set up for capturing it.

'Yes, by all means approach the *panchayat*. Let it be settled. I too do not much appreciate these daily bickering.'

Who would win the suit in the *panchayat*: about that Jumman did not have the least doubt. Who was there in all the neighbouring villages who was not indebted to him for some favour or the other; who was there who would dare to take animosity with him. After all the angels were not going to descend from the heavens to participate in the *panchayat!*

II

For a number of days after the above incident, the old aunt kept running around in the neighbouring villages with a walking stick in hand. Her back was bent like a bow, it was difficult for her to take each step; but then it had come to such an end. It was necessary that the issue be resolved.

There was hardly anyone before whom the old woman had not shed her tears of sadness. Some simply agreed with her in a superficial manner; others cursed the world for this type of injustice. Some said, 'She has one foot in the grave; she may die any day; yet the yearning for money does not go! Now what do you require, just eat your bread and pray to God. What would you do with land and such things?' There were some persons who found it a good occasion to indulge in humour. An arched backbone, a soft hollow face, white hair that looked like straw; how could one not find it humourous when so many of these elements were to be found together? There were very few kind and gentle hearted person who favoured justice and who heard the sad tale of the helpless woman carefully and gave her some reassurance. After going around everywhere the poor woman came to Algu and throwing away her stick and taking a few breaths, she said, 'Son you too come for a while to the *panchayat*.'

'Why do you want me to come? People from various villages would be there in any case.'

'I have gone around everywhere telling them my sad tale. Whether to come or not is in their hands.'

'All right I will come for the sake of it; but I will not open my mouth in the *panchayat*.'

'Why son?'

'Now what do I answer to that? My own sweet will. Jumman is an old friend of mine. I cannot afford to spoil my relationship with him.'

'Why my son, for fear of spoiling relationship would you not speak the truth?'

If our sleeping conscience is robbed of all its wealth, it would not even notice it; however it gets aroused if it is challenged and then nothing can conquer it. Algu could not give her an answer but her words kept ringing in his mind, 'for fear of spoiling relationship would you not speak the truth'

III

The *panchayat* assembled under a tree in the evening. Shaikh Jumman had already got a carpet spread. He had also made arrangements for *pan*, cardamom, *hukkah* and tobacco. However, he himself was sitting a little away from Chowdhary Algu. Whenever someone would approach the *panchayt* he would welcome him with a mild bow. After the sun had set and the congregation of sparrows started it clamour on the trees, the *panchayat* below also commenced. The carpet was fully covered but most of the people present were mere onlookers. Among the invited gentlemen only those had arrived who had some score to settle with Jumman. A fire was smouldering in one corner from which the village barber was constantly filling the *chillums* for the *hukkahs*. It was impossible to decide if the smouldering cow dung cakes were emitting more smoke or the exhalations made by those drawing on the *chillums*. Young boys were running around here and there. Some were abusing each other, some were crying. There was quite a clamour all around. The village dogs had gathered in hordes mistaking the gathering for a feast.

After the *panchas* sat down the old aunt made her submissions,

'*Panchas*, it is three years since I transferred all my land in the name of my nephew Jumman. You would already know about it that Jumman had solemnly agreed to provide me food and raiment. I have somehow spent over a year with him crying and suffering every day. Now I cannot bear this bickering that takes place every day, any more. I neither get sufficient food nor proper clothing. I am a helpless widow. I cannot take recourse to a court of law. Now where else do I tell my tale of woe except in front of you? Whatever way you decide, I will abide with that. If you find anything wrong in me you may give a slap on my face. If you find anything wrong with Jumman, advise him; why does he invite the wrath of an old hapless woman. The order that you *panchas* give will be binding on me.'

Ramdhan Mishra, to many of whose tenant farmers Jumman had given refuge in his village said, 'Jumman *mian*[28] whom do you nominate as *panch*? Decide right now, for afterwards whatever the *panchas* say will have to be accepted by you.'

Jumman could espy among the people who were present, only those with whom he had some animosity for some reason or the other. He said, 'An order given by the *panchas* is like the order of Allah. Let my dear aunt nominate anyone she wishes. I have no objection.'

The aunt said in a loud voice, 'For the sake of Allah, why don't you tell the names of the *panchas*? At least let me know what you want.'

Jumman replied in anger, 'Don't make me open my mouth now. It is you who is aggrieved, nominate as *panchas* whomsoever you want.'

The aunt could understand what was in his mind and said, 'Son, have some fear of God, a *panch* is neither your friend nor your enemy. What are trying to say? If you don't have faith on anyone then leave them; you have regard at least for Algu Chowdhary? Here, I name him only as the chief *panch*.'

Jumman was full of joy but hiding his feelings he said, 'Let it be Algu, for me both Algu and Ramdhan are alike.'

Algu did not want to get embroiled in this dispute. He tried to excuse himself saying, 'Aunt you know I am a close friend of Jumman.'

'Son, one doesn't give up one's principles for the sake of friendship. God himself resides in the heart of a *panch*. Whatever comes out of the mouth of a *panch* is the voice of God himself.'

Algu was appointed as the head of the *panchas*. Ramdhan Mishra and other opponents of Jumman cursed the old aunt in their mind.

Algu Chowdhary said, 'Shakih Jumman, you and I are old friends! When needed you helped me and I too have been serving you to the best of my ability; however, at this moment you and your old aunt are equal in our eyes. You may submit to the *panchas* whatever you desire to say.'

Jumman was convinced that it was his day. Whatever Algu had just said was just a charade. Therefore with a cool mind he said, '*Panchas*, three years back my aunt had transferred her land in my name. I had agreed to provide her food and clothing during all her life. God is witness that till this day I have not caused any discomfort to my dear aunt. I consider her like my mother. It is my duty to serve her, but there is some discord among the womenfolk. How can I be responsible for that? My aunt demands in addition, a monthly allowance. How much was the land in question is known to all. There is not so much profit arising from it that I could give her a monthly allowance. Moreover, there was no reference to monthly allowance in the transfer deed. Otherwise I would never have got into this tangle. That is about all I have to say. The *panchas,* otherwise, have the right to decide the matter in the manner they like.'

Algu Chowdhary had to deal quite often with the court. He was therefore well versed with legal matters. He started the argument with Jumman. Each question fell like the blow of hammer on the heart of Jumman. Ramdhan Mishra was feeling spellbound by those questions. Jumman was feeling utterly surprised about what had happened to Algu. 'It is just a little while back that he was sitting with me and talking all kind of things. What has happened to him so suddenly that he is bent on digging out my roots[29]? What it that he is taking this revenge for is, I wonder. Would such a long friendship too be of no avail?'

Jumman Sheikh was still lost in these thoughts; when Algu announced the decision, 'Jumman Sheikh! The *panchas* have given their serious consideration to this issue. It appears reasonable to them that your aunt be provided with a monthly allowance for her expenses. We are of the view that her land surely yields enough revenue for an allowance to be paid. Now, that is our decision; if it is not acceptable to Jumman to provide such allowance then the gift deed may be treated as annulled.'

Jumman was stunned to hear that decision. 'He, who was supposed to be your friend behaving like your enemy and putting the dagger to your throat; what shall one call that except vagaries of time? He in whom you reposed absolute trust deceives you right when you need him. It is on such occasions alone that true or false friends are tested. This is what friendship has come to in these evil times. If people were not so deceptive and dishonest then why would there be all kind of maladies in the country? All these diseases like cholera, plagues etc are nothing but punishments for such wicked deeds.'

However Ramdhan Mishra and other *panchas* were praising Algu Chowdhary for his devotion to justice. 'He has separated the milk from water and water from the milk![30] Friendship is at its own place, but what is more important is to follow the right path of justice. It is on the strength of such upright persons alone that the earth is able to support itself; otherwise it would have sunk long back into the deep abyss of hell.'

That decision shook the foundation of Jumman and Algu's friendship. Now they were not to be seen any more talking to each other. Such an old tree of friendship could not face even one blast of the wind of truth. It seemed to be standing on a bed of fine sand indeed. Courteousness now became more pronounced in their conduct. They became more hospitable to each other. They would meet but in the manner a sword meets a shield.

In the mind of Jumman the deceitfulness of his friend would keep on nagging the whole day. The only thing that preoccupied his mind all the time now was how to find an occasion to take revenge.

IV

It takes a long time to accomplish a good task but it is not always so when it comes to accomplishing a bad deed. Jumman too found the occasion to settle his score quite soon. A year earlier, Algu Chowdhary had bought a fine pair of bullocks. The bullocks were of a fine western breed and had long horns. For months people from neighbouring villages had kept coming to see them. It so transpired that one month after Jumman's *panchayat* had taken place, one of the bullocks died. 'It is the retribution for his treachery' said Jumman to his friends, 'A man may reconcile and seek solace but the just God witnesses everything.'

Algu had a suspicion that Jumman had poisoned the bullock. His wife too laid the charge for the mishap on Jumman. 'Jumman has played some foul trick,' she alleged. One day there was a lengthy argument between the wives of Algu and Jumman. Both the ladies made rivers of copious verbiage to flow. Sarcasm, innuendo, allegory, simile and many other figures of speech were employed in the conversation. Jumman somehow restored the peace. He reprimanded his wife and pacified her and took her away from the battle zone. Algu Chowdhary, on the other hand, took recourse to the baton of logical reasoning to bring his wife back to sense.

Of what use can be a sole bullock? Efforts were therefore made to find a match for it but without any success. So it was decided that it should be sold off. There was one Samjhu Sahu in the village, who ran a cart drawn by a single bullock. He used to carry jaggery and refined butter from the village to the nearby marketplace and bring back salt and oils from there for selling in the village. He took a fancy for the bullock. He thought that if he could lay a hand on that bullock he would easily make three trips in a day. At present, he was finding it difficult to make even one round. He examined the bullock, made it run his cart, bargained over the price and did not rest till he had brought it home and tied it to the peg outside his doorstep. It was agreed to make the payment in one month. Algu Chowdhary was in need of a customer; he did not care for any loss.

When Samjhu found a new bullock he started making it toil. He started making two, even three rounds every day. He would not be concerned about its fodder or water, all that mattered to him was number of trips.

He would take it to the market and throw some dry hay in front of it. The poor animal would not have time even to regain its breath when it would be put to the yoke once again. When it was at Algu's place it had a comfortable time. It would be only once in a while that it would be brought to the yoke and then it would run merrily for miles together. There the prized bullock was served clear water, ground lentils and mustard cake along with hay and that was not all; once in a while it would get to taste even ghee. Every morning and evening someone would rub its skin, wipe it and message it. It was just peace and tranquillity there, whereas now it was sheer drudgery for it the entire day. After merely a month, the bullock started looking emaciated. He would get into a fright the moment he saw the yoke of the cart. Every step would be a challenge for it. Its bones had started showing; yet it was a proud bullock that was not used to getting whipped.

One day during the fourth round Sahuji loaded twice the luggage in the cart. After an entire days labour the poor, tired animal was finding it difficult to take even one step. But Sahuji started whipping him. What could he do, the poor animal; he made a desperate effort and started moving. It ran for a while and then thought of taking a little rest but Sahuji was in a hurry to reach back; so he wielded the whipped heartlessly a number of times. The poor bullock made yet another effort but its strength had given way. It fell down and it could not get up thereafter. Sahuji kept hitting for a long time then pulled its leg, put his stick into its nose but can a dead being get up? It was then that Sahuji had a doubt. He looked carefully at the bullock and then detached it from the yoke and then started wondering how the cart would reach home. He kept shouting for a long time but the village roads are like the eyes of an infant; they close down as soon as it is evening. He could not see anyone around. There was no village in the vicinity. Full of anger, he started cursing the dead bullock, 'Wretched beast! If he had to die he could have waited at least till we had reached home. But he had to die right in the middle of the journey. Now who is going to pull the cart? Sahuji kept squirming and fuming in anger in that manner. He had sold a number of sacs of jaggery and canisters of ghee in the market and had two three hundred rupees in his pocket. Apart from that there were so many sacs of salt in the cart; he could not go away leaving those unguarded. Feeling helpless, he lay down in his cart and decided to spend the night there itself. He made a *chillum* for himself and after some time he tried his hookah. In this manner he kept himself engaged till mid night. He thought he had remained awake the entire night but when he woke up at day break, he found his purse was missing. He looked around in despair and found that a number of oil canisters were also missing! Feeling sad he struck his head and started writhing in grief. In the morning he reached home almost crying. When his wife heard the bad news, first she cried and then she started cursing and abusing Algu Chowdhary, 'The wretch gave us such an ominous bullock that we have lost our earnings of a lifetime.'

Many months passed after this incident. Whenever Algu asked for the price of his bullock both the Sahu and his wife would jump at his neck like mad dogs and start speaking irrelevant things, 'Here we have lost our life's earnings, we have got ruined and he is bothered only about his price. First he gave us a dead bullock and on top of that he is asking for its price. He made a fool of us and tied that cursed bullock around our neck! Do you think we are idiots? We too also *banias*[31]; if you are looking for nincompoops you would find them elsewhere. First go and wash your face in some ditch than demand your price. If you can't help it, take our bullock and use it for two months in place of one. What else can you ask for?'

There was no dearth of ill wishers of Chowdhary Algu. On such occasions they would gather and endorse Sahuji's gibberish. But it was not easy to give up one hundred fifty rupees like that. Once he too lost temper. Sahuji took offense and went inside the house looking for a stick. In the meanwhile, his wife took over the defence. Arguments soon led to a scuffle. Hearing the noise the people of the village assembled. They advised both of them. 'It cannot go on in this manner. Call a *panchayat*. Whatever is decided there accept that.' Sahuji agreed. Algu also affirmed that.

V

Preparations began for the *panchayat*. Both the sides started finding their supporters. Three days after, the *panchayat* was held under the same tree. It was the same hour in the evening. In the fields the crows were having their own *panchayat*. The matter of dispute was whether they have any right over the peanuts that grow there; and till the time that question was solved they considered it their right to express their displeasure at the shouting of the watchman. The company of parrots sitting on the branches of the tree were debating the issue whether human beings had any right to call them ungrateful when they themselves do not shy away from betraying their friends.

When the *panchayat* was ready, Ramdhan Mishra asked, 'Now what is there to delay about? Let the *panchas* be selected. Say Chowdhary, who all do you nominate as *panchas*?'

Algu said in a humble tone, 'let Samjhu Sahu select them himself.'

Samjhu got up and said in a booming voice, 'From my side Jumman Shaikh.'

The moment Algu heard the name of Jumman his heart started beating as if someone had struck a sudden blow to him. Ramdhan was a friend of Algu. He fathomed what he had in mind and asked, 'You don't have any objection to that Algu?'

'No what objection may I have,' said Algu losing all hope.

VI

The awareness of our responsibility is often a remedy for our narrow minded conduct. When we start wandering after losing our way then it is this very knowledge that becomes our trustworthy guide.

The editor of a newspaper sitting in his quiet chamber attacks so irreverently and independently the council of ministers; however an occasion arises when he himself is a part of the council of ministers. How incisive, how thoughtful and justice oriented his pen becomes all of a sudden, the moment he steps into the council building. The reason for that is the awareness of one's responsibility. How boisterous a man is during his youth? How worried his parents feel about him. They may think him as a curse to the family; however after a very short period, once the responsibility of the household is thrust on his shoulders that disorganized and impatient young man transforms into such a patient and serene person: this too is the result of the awareness of one's responsibilities.

After he occupied the place of the *sarpanch*, in Jumman Shaikh's mind also a sense of responsibility came into being. 'At this moment I am sitting at the supreme seat of justice and morality,' he thought, 'Whatever comes out from my mouth is akin to the voice of god and in the voice of god there can be no place for my personal feelings. I should not budge even a small bit from the truth.'

The *panchas* began asking questions from both the parties. Both the sides kept defending themselves for a long time. Everyone agreed on the point that Samjhu Sahu should pay the price of the bullock. However two gentlemen wanted some concession on the ground that Samjhu suffered loss due to the death of the bullock. As against this two persons also wanted to punish Samjhu so that no one would dare to treat their animal in such a heartless manner. In the end Jumman announced his decision:

'Algu Chowdhary and Samjhu Sahu! The *panchas* have carefully considered your matter. It would be appropriate that Samjhu pays the full price of the bullock. At the time when he bought the bullock it did not suffer from any infirmity. Had the price been paid at that time itself

Samjhu could not have demanded it back. The death of the bullock took place because it was made to do immense labour and proper arrangement was not made for its fodder.'

Ramdhan Mishra said, 'Samjhu has intentionally killed the bullock, therefore he must be penalised for that.'

'That is a separate question. We are not concerned with it.'

Jhagdu Sahu said, 'Some concession should be made for Samjhu.'

'That depends on Algu Chowdhary. If he makes some concession it would be kind of him' replied Jumman.

Algu Chowdhary could not contain his joy. He got up and said loudly, 'Long live the *panch parmeshwar*!'

Everyone was full of praise for Jumman's decision. 'This is called justice! It is not the act of a human being; it is the gift of god who resides in the mind of the *panch*. Who can say a wrong is right before the *panch*?'

After a while Jumman came to Algu and embracing him said, 'Brother, ever since you had conducted my *panchayat*, I had become your sworn enemy, but today I realized that a person occupying the seat of a *panch* can be neither anyone's friend nor his enemy. He cannot think of anything else but justice. Today I have got convinced that god himself speaks through the mouth of the *panch*. Algu started crying. His tears washed away the grime that had accumulated in the heart of both of them. The vine of friendship that had dried up became green once again.

The Shroud

The father and son both sat silently near the doorstep of the hut in front of a dying fire. Inside the young wife of the son was writhing in labour pain. Every now and then such a heart rending cry would come out of her mouth that would make both of them hold their arms firmly against their chest. It was a winter night, the nature was submerged in silence and the entire village was covered by darkness.

'It appears that she will not survive. The entire day has gone by, go at least take a look at her,' said Ghishu.

Madhav got offended and said, 'If she has to die why does she not do so? What will I get by looking at her?'

'You are very heartless, you wretch. Such disloyalty towards her with whom you have lived so contentedly for an entire year!'

'I cannot bear her twisting and turning in pain and throwing her hands and legs around.'

It was a family of hide makers which was notorious in the village. Ghishu, if he worked for one year, he would relax for three days. As for Madhav he was such a shirker that he would work for half an hour and then smoke chillum for an hour. It was because of this that they did not find any work. If there were even a handful of grain available at home, it would be out of question for them to go out for work. Only after they would be forced to skip a few meals, Ghisu would climb a tree and break some branches and Madhav would go and sell them and thereafter as long as the money would last they would loiter around here and there.

There was no dearth of work in the village. It was a village of farmers; there were scores of jobs available for a hard working person. However these two would be called only when someone would have no option but to make do with the output of one person while employing two. Had both of them been ascetics they would not need to practice self discipline and orderliness in life to attain patience and contentment as that was their very nature.

Theirs was a bizarre existence. They had nothing by way of possessions at home except for a few earthen pots. As for clothes, they were carrying on with their lives with tattered and torn clothes just enough to cover their nudity. Though free from all worldly cares they were loaded with debt. They would suffer abuses, even blows but had no worry about it. They looked so pathetic that despite complete absence of any hope for recovery, people would still give them some loan however petty it may be. During the season of potatoes and peas, they would pluck some potatoes or peas and eat them after roasting them or they would pluck a few sugar canes and chew them during the night.

Ghisu had spent sixty years of his live living in this manner and Madhav too was following in the footsteps of his father, like a true son; in fact he was making his name even more illustrious. At this moment too both were sitting in front of a fire and baking some potatoes that they had dug out of someone's field. Ghishu's wife had died long back. Madahv had got married a year earlier. Ever since that woman had arrived she had laid the foundation of orderliness in the family and had been taking care of both the shameless persons. They had become even more comfort loving since then. In fact they had even started putting on airs a little. If someone sent for them for work, they would ask double the wages. Today the same woman was dying of labour pangs and both of them were awaiting her death, so that they could sleep peacefully.

'At least go and take a look at her, in what state she is? She must be ridden with evil spirits. Here even a witch doctor would ask for one rupee' said Ghishu taking out a potato and peeling it.

Madahv apprehended that if he went inside the hut then Ghisu might finish a big amount of potatoes. He said, 'I feel scared of going inside.'

'What are you scared of, I am here after all.'

'So you may take a look yourself.'

'When my wife died I had not moved away from her for three days. And won't she feel shy of me? Should I see the uncovered body of her's whose face even I have not seen till today? She won't even be conscious of her body. If she sees me she would not even be able to throw her hand and feet in peace.'

'What will happen if she gives birth to a child, I wonder? Jaggery, oil, grain there is nothing whatsoever in the house.'

'Everything will come. Provided god gives her a child. Those very people who are not giving us even a paisa today will call us tomorrow and give us rupees. I had nine sons. I would have nothing at home but with the grace of god I somehow sailed through.'

In a society in which, even those who toil day and night were no better off and compared to those farmers they who knew how to make profit from the farmers are much more prosperous, it is not surprising that such a mentality develops itself. We would say that Ghisu was much more of a thinker than the farmers and instead of joining the ignorant horde of farmers he had joined the vile company of idlers. Indeed he did not have the capacity to observe the rules and policies of the idlers. Therefore, while some others of that company had become the leaders and headmen of villages, everyone pointed a finger at him. Yet he had at least the satisfaction that even though he was a pauper he did not have to go through drudgery like those farmers and that others were not able to take undue advantage of his simplicity and helplessness.

Both of them started taking out the hot potatoes and eating them even though they were still piping hot. They had not eaten anything since yesterday. Neither of them had the patience to allow the potatoes to become a little cool. Their tongues got burnt many times. After their skins were peeled off the potato scorched the tongue as well the throat and it was better to ensure that it reached inside instead of letting it remain in the mouth. They were therefore swallowing them quickly though in the process tears would come out of their eyes.

Ghisu remembered at that moment the wedding of the *thakur*[32] that he had been to some twenty years back. The satiation that he had derived during that feast was something memorable in his life. Even today that memory was fresh in his mind. 'I can't forget that feast. Ever since that day never again have I had that kind of food and that too bellyful of it. The girl's side made everyone eat *poouris*[33] to their hearts' content...everyone! Big or small everyone had *poouris* and that too made in real ghee! *chutni*[34], *raita*[35], three types of dry vegetables, one vegetable with curry, curd and *mithai*[36]. Now how do I explain to you how savoury the food was and there was no limit; ask for whatever you like, eat as much as you like. People ate so much, so much, that no one could drink water. But those serving you were such that they would keep pouring round, hot *poouris* in your *pattal*[37]. You keep telling them that you don't want any more, you keep covering your *pattal* with your hands, but they would keep giving. And when everyone had washed his mouth, there was cardamom and *pan*. As for me where was the energy left to think of a *pan*? I could not even get up. I went and lay down quickly on my blanket. He was such a generous hearted man that *thakur*!'

Making an effort to enjoy those delicacies in his imagination, Madhav said, 'Now no one calls you to such a feast.'

'Who would do that now? Those were different times. Now everyone thinks of economizing. Don't spend money on marriage, don't spend money on funerals. Ask them where they will keep all that money that they wrest from the poor? There is no let up in that extortion. Yes when it comes to spending it they think of economizing.'

'You must have had twenty *poouris*?'

'I ate more than twenty.'

'I would have eaten fifty.'

'I would not have had less than fifty. I was really hefty. You are not even half of what I used to be.'

After finishing the potatoes both of them drank some water and covering themselves with their dhotis and curling up their legs against their stomach they went to sleep there itself in front of the fire. It was as if they were two coiled up pythons lying there.

And Budhia was still moaning.

II

In the morning Madhav went inside the hut and found that his wife had become cold. Flies were hovering on her face. Eyes that looked like stones were stretched upwards. The entire body was covered with dust. The child had died in the womb.

Madhav came running to Ghishu. Then both of them started wailing loudly and beating their breasts. When the neighbours head their crying, they came running and started consoling the wretches in the customary fashion.

However it was not the time for wailing and howling. The shroud and wood for the pyre had to be arranged. Money was missing in the house like meat in the nest of a vulture.

The father and son went crying to the *zamindar*, the headman of the village. He used to hate even their faces. They had been beaten up by him many times: for stealing, for not turning up for work in spite of promising to do so.

'Why Ghisua why are you crying?' Now a days you are not even to be seen! It seems you don't want to live any more in this village.'

Ghisu put his head on the floor and with eyes full of tears said, 'I am in great adversity my lord. Madhav's wife passed away last night. She kept suffering the entire night my lord. Both of us were sitting beside her; we gave her whatever treatment we could arrange, did whatever we could for her, yet she left us. Now there is no one left even to make food for us, my lord! We are ruined. Our household is wrecked. I am your slave. Now who else except for you would help us in arranging for her last rites? Whatever we had has gone in her treatment. Now only if you have mercy on us than her dead body would be lifted. Except for you whose doorstep may I go to now?'

The headman was kind hearted. But to be kind to someone like Ghishu too was not very appropriate. He felt like driving him away and telling him that he never turned up whenever he needed him, even after he was summoned and now that he needs help he was being so servile, the wretch, good for nothing fellow! However it was no occasion to show anger or to mete out punishment. Even though he was feeling irritated, he took out two rupees and threw them at him. However he did not utter one word of consolation. He did not even look at him. It was as if he had got rid of a burden.

When the village headman had given two rupees, how could the village traders and moneylenders dare to refuse? Ghisu, moreover, wanted to drop the name of the headman all over. Someone gave two *annas*[38], some four *annas*. In one hour Ghisu had collected a tidy sum of five rupees. Someone gave a little grain, someone a little wood. So in the afternoon Ghishu and Madhav left for the bazaar to purchase a shroud. Some people had started chopping bamboos and wood for the pyre. Soft hearted women of the village came to see the dead body and shed a tear or two before they left.

III

When they reached the bazaar, Ghisu asked, 'As for wood, there seem to be enough to cremate her, isn't it Madhav?'

'Yes there is enough wood, now we need a shroud.'

'So let's go and buy some inexpensive type of a shroud.'

'Yes, by the time the dead body would be lifted it will be night. Who is going to notice the shroud in the night?'

'What a stupid custom—even he who did not have a rag to cover his body needs a new shroud when he dies.'

'The shroud gets brunt with the dead body.'

'Yes of course, you think it gets preserved? Had we found these five rupees earlier, we could have arranged for some medicine for her.'

Both of them could fathom each other's mind. They kept roaming around in the bazaar. They would go to one cloth shop and then to the other! They looked at different kinds of cloth: silk, cotton but nothing appealed to them. It went on and on up to the time when it was evening. At that time due as if to some divine inspiration they found themselves in front of a bar. And as if it was predestined, they entered it. They stood around for some time in a state of indecision. Then Ghisu approached the counter and said, 'Sahuji please give us a bottle too.'

After that some salty snacks was ordered, followed by some fried fish and both of them went and sat quietly in the veranda and started drinking. After gulping down quickly a few drinks both of them got inebriated.

'Of what avail would be the shroud? After all it has to get burnt. Nothing would have gone with her.'

Madahv looked towards the sky, as if making the gods a witness to his impartiality, 'That is the way of the world, otherwise why do people give thousands of rupees to the *brahmins*? Who is able to see if one gets anything in the other world?'

'The rich have got money, let them burn it. What do we have to burn?'

'But what will you tell the people? They will ask where the shroud is.'

Ghisu laughed and said 'We will tell them that we lost the money. That we searched a lot but could not find it. The people won't believe it, but they themselves will give money once again.'

Madhav also laughed at the unanticipated stroke of luck and said, 'she was really a good soul; even when she died she ensured that we were well fed.'

More than half the bottle had vanished. Ghishu ordered two *seers*[39] of *poouries*, *chutni*, pickle and liver from the shop in front of the bar. Madhav went and brought all that with alacrity. One and half rupees were spent. Now just a little bit of change remained.

Both of them were sitting and eating the *poouries* proudly as if some lion was devouring his prey in a jungle. They were not worried about their responsibility nor were they bothered about ignominy. They had conquered those feelings long back.

Ghisu said in a philosophical vein, 'If we are getting so much pleasure won't she get some merit for it?'

Madhav lowered his head in a sign of respect and made a wish, 'God you are omnipresent, take her to heaven. Both of us are giving her blessings with our heart. This food that we have got today, we had never had something like that earlier in life.'

After a while Madhav had a doubt, 'Tell me *dada*, we too will go there one day or the other.'

Ghishu did not reply to that innocent query. He did not want to put any obstruction in his pleasure by thinking of the other world.

'What will you tell them if someone asks why we did not get the shroud?'

'We will tell them nothing.'

'But they will ask for sure.'

'How do you know that she will not get a shroud? You think I am an ass? I have not spent sixty years of my life for nothing. She will get a shroud and a very good one!'

Madhav could not believe him. He said, 'Who will give her that? You have spent all the money. It is me she would ask. It was I who married her.'

'Tell me, why don't you say anything?'

'Those very people will give who gave us this time, though this time the money will not reach our hands.'

As the darkness increased and the lustre of the stars increased, the bar too became livelier. Someone sang, someone bragged, someone was embracing his friend and someone was sticking his glass to the mouth of his companion.'

The environment itself was intoxicating; the air was full of excitement. So many people had got drunk with just a palm-full of drink after arriving here. More than liquor it was the environment that had an intoxicating effect on them. The constraints of life drew them here and for a little while they would forget if they were living or dead.

Both father and son were still sipping their drinks with great enjoyment. Everyone's eyes were focused on them. How fortunate to have one full bottle between two of them!

After having his fill Madhav gave the plate made of dried leaves, containing the rest of the *poouris* to a beggar who stood there eyeing them with famished eyes. Madhav experienced for the first time in his life the pride and exuberance of giving something.

'Take it and eat as much as you want and give your blessing,' said Ghishu, 'she to whom these earnings belonged is dead. However your good wishes would indeed reach her. Give your blessing from all corners of your heart; it was really hard earned money.'

Madhav looked again towards the heavens and said, 'She would go to *Vaikunth*[40] dada, she will become the queen of *Vaikunth*.'

Ghishu stood up and feeling as if he had been swimming in the waves of euphoria, he said, 'Yes my son she will go to *Vaikunth*. She never persecuted anyone, never bullied anyone. Even as she died she fulfilled the greatest desire of our life. If she does not go to *Vaikunth* would these fat people go there who rob the poor with both their hands and then make offerings in the temples and take dips in Ganges to wipe away their sins.

Those feelings of reverence got over soon. Instability is the principal trait of intoxication. The phase of sadness and disappointment took over.

Madhav said, 'But *dada*, the poor one suffered so much in her life. How much agony she endured before she died!'

Covering his eyes with his palms he started weeping, howling loudly.

Ghisu consoled him, 'Why are you crying son, be happy that she got free from this maze of artificiality; rid herself of this web of lies. She was indeed fortunate to have broken away from the fetters of attachment and illusion.'

Both of them started singing a song:

'Oh cheater, why do you roll around your eyes! You cheater.'

The eyes of all the drunkards were focused on them and these two were singing merrily to their heart's content. Then they started dancing. They jumped and pranced. They fell and then got up and swayed around. They indulged in little bit of acting. In the end they collapsed there itself overwhelmed by intoxication.

Mother

Today the prisoner is coming home after getting released. Karuna had already tidied up the house one day in advance. During these three years whatever five ten rupees she had saved after struggling hard had all been spent on the preparations for the welcome and hospitality of the husband. She bought a new pair of *dhoties*[41], got new *kurtas*[42] stitched; for the child she arranged for a new coat and a cap. She was embracing the child again and again and feeling happy. Had this child not appeared like the sun to brighten up her sombre life, perhaps the blows of misfortune that she had received might have put an end to her life. Three months after her husband was sentenced to prison this child was born. She had passed those three years looking at his face. How happy he would be when I take the child to him, she thought, he would be amazed to see him and then take him in his lap and say. 'Karun you had done me such a favour by giving me this jewel.' Listening to the babbling of the child, he would forget all those sufferings he went through in the prison; one simple, pure and charming look of his would clean up his heart. Imagining this, her heart was swelling with pleasure.

She was thinking there would be a lot of people with Aditya. When he reaches the doorstep it would resound with the sounds of people hailing his arrival. How heavenly a view it would be! She had spread out a carpet for them, which looked somewhat worn out, made some *pans* and was looking repeatedly towards the doorstep expectantly. The image of her sturdy, kind and energetic husband came to her mind now and then. She remembered again and again the words he had said when he had left, his fortitude and self confidence that remained undaunted even faced with the blows of the policemen; that smile that was still fresh on his lips, that self dignity that still reflected from his visage. Could that ever be effaced from the mind of Karuna! As she remembered that a red tint of self pride covered the lifeless face of Karuna. It was that very support that fortified her heart during the intense anguish that she suffered during three years. So many nights she had to fast; often there would not be even a lamp to light the house, but had never happened that tears of helplessness would come out from her eyes. Today all those misfortunes would come to an end. She would face everything with a smile in the strong embrace of her husband. She would have no wishes left once she had those immense riches.

The age old traveller of the celestial path was moving towards its resting place, where evening had spread its golden carpet covered with layer of bright flowers. At that moment Karuna noticed a man coming near supporting himself with a walking stick that sounded like the mournful voice of a worn out man. After every few steps he would stop and start coughing. His head was bent; Karuna could not see his face, but from his bearing he appeared to be some old man. However, when he came nearer in a while Karuna recognised him. That was her dear husband indeed but alas, how transformed his visage had become. That youth, that radiance, that agility and that well-built physique all that had vanished. Only a skeleton of bones remained. There was neither any companion nor any friend accompanying him. Karuna came out immediately as soon as she recognised him, but that desire to get into his embrace remained suppressed in her heart. All her hopes were dashed and mingled with dirt. Her euphoria flowed out in a flow of tears and got vanished.

Aditya looked towards her as he entered and smiled. Nevertheless that smile contained in itself an enormous pain. Karuna became immobile as if her heartbeat had come to a stop. She was gazing with eyes wide open towards her husband as if she could not believe her eyes. Not a word of welcome or of sadness came out of her mouth. The child, sitting in her lap too looked apprehensively towards that skeleton and tried to cling on to her.

Finally she said in a pained voice, 'What is this state you have got into? You have become unrecognizable.'

Aditya made an effort to smile trying to allay her fears—it is nothing, I have just lost some weight. Once I eat the food made by you I will regain my health once again.'

'You have become so thin. Did you not get enough food there? You used to say that political prisoners are treated well and what happened to your friends who used to surround you the whole day and who would be ready to shed blood for you.'

Aditya's brows got creased as he said, 'It has been a very bitter experience Karuna! I did not know that they would turn away their eyes from me once I got arrested and then no one would bother anymore for me. I didn't know this would be the reward you get for being ready to sacrifice yourself for the nation. That people forget their servants very soon I knew; but one's colleagues and supporters can be so unfaithful—that I experienced for the first time. However I have no complaint against anyone. Service in itself is its reward. It was my mistake that I wished for fame and renown too in return.'

'So you did not get enough food there?'

'Don't ask me that Karuna, it is a very sad story. It is sufficient that I have come back alive. I was to see your face once again; otherwise I bore such hardship that by now I should have departed from the world. I will lie down for a while. I can't stand, I have walked so much today.'

'Come eat something first before you lie down. See he is you *babuji*[43] my son, your *babuji*' she said picking up the child, 'go and sit in his lap, he will play with you.'

Aditya looked at the child with eyes full of tears and his entire being started reprimanding himself. He was not so sorry for the state of his decrepit body. With god's grace, if he recovers he would never ever go near the national movement. But what right he had to bring that innocent child into the world and throw him into the fire of poverty? Now he would start worshipping the goddess Lakshmi and dedicate himself to the upbringing of his child. He felt at that time as if the child was looking at him with contempt, as if saying, 'Which responsibility did you fulfill towards me?' He was eager with his whole heart to pick up and embrace the child but he was not able to raise his hands. There was not enough power left in those hands.

Karuna got up with the child in her hands and brought some food in a plate. Aditya looked with hungry eyes towards the plate as if it was after many days that he had seen something to eat. He knew that after fasting for a number of days and in his present worn out state of health he should control himself. But he could not do so; he grabbed the plate and devoured the food in no time. Karuna was feeling a little doubtful. She did not ask if he would have anything more. She picked up the plate and walked away.

'He never used to eat so much,' she said to herself.

Karuna was feeding the child, when she suddenly heard, 'Karuna.'

She went to him and asked, 'Did you call me.'

Aditya's face had turned yellow and he was breathing very fast. He had lied down on the carpet itself. Karuna became apprehensive looking at his state, 'Shall I go and call some doctor.'

Aditya waved his hand and said, 'It is of no use Karuna. Now it is no use to hide from you, I am suffering from tuberculosis. I have escaped death more than once. I was destined to see you people; that alone kept me alive. Look my dear, don't cry.'

Karuna suppressed her sobs and said, 'I will be back soon with the doctor.'

Aditya shook his head, 'No Karuna, just keep sitting with me. I have no hope left from anyone. The doctors have given up. What surprises me is how I have managed to reach here. I don't know which divine power has been able to draw me from there. Perhaps it is the last flicker of this lamp. Oh, I have done great injustice to you. I will always feel sorry for that! I could never give you any comfort...could not do anything for you. I am leaving you after merely putting the taint of marriage on you and leaving you with the responsibility of bringing up a child. Oh!'

'Are you having any pain? Shall I make some fire to warm you? Why don't you say something?'

Aditya turned to the other side and said, 'No need to do anything dear. I don't have any pain. I only feel as if my heart is coming to a standstill, as if I am drowning in water. The story of my life is coming to an end. I can see the lamp getting extinguished. I can't tell when my voice will stop. I want to tell you whatever I have to say; why take away that desire with me. Would you answer a question of mine...shall I ask?'

It seemed the entire weakness in Karuna's mind, her entire sorrow and grief had disappeared and in its place a self confidence was born which laughs at death and plays with the snakes of misfortune. The way a sharp sword remains hidden in a velvet scabbard with precious stones woven in it, the way immense energy remains hidden in the gentle flow of water, the tender heart of a woman keeps hidden immense courage and patience inside it. The way anger makes one draw the sword out of the scabbard, the way science is able to harness the power of water, in the same manner love ignites the courage and fortitude in a woman.

Karuna kept her hand on her huband's head and said, 'why don't you ask my dear?'

Aditya felt the tender contact of Karuna's hand and said, 'In your view how was my life? Was it worth anything to talk about? See, you had never hidden anything from me. Now also say it clearly. In your view should I laugh over my life or cry over it?'

Karuna said with joy, 'Why do you ask this question, dear? Have I every disregarded you? You life had been like that of gods: totally unselfish, detached and ideal. Upset due to various impediments in life, so many times I had tried to draw you towards worldliness. That time in my heart I knew that I am trying to make you fall from a high pedestal. Had you fallen into the trap of desires and illusions of life I would perhaps had been more satisfied, but my soul would not feel that pride and elation that I am feeling now. If I could bestow on anyone the greatest blessing it would be that his life should be like yours.

As she said that her lustreless face started glowing as if it had become divine. Aditya looked with proud eyes towards Karuna and said, 'That's all, now I am satisfied Karuna. I am not worried about this child; I could not leave him in abler hands. I am convinced that during your entire life this high and pure ideal would always remain before you. I am prepared to die now.'

II

Seven years passed by. The child, Prakash was now a ten year old handsome, strong and smiling youth. He was strong and agile, courageous and high-thinking. As for fear it did not come anywhere near him. Karuna's grief-stricken heart used to get comforted seeing him. People might consider Karuna to be unfortunate or helpless. However she never complained about her destiny. She sold her ornaments that were dearer to her than her life when her husband was alive and with that money she purchased a few cows and buffalos. She was the daughter of a farmer; therefore, looking after cows was nothing new for her. She made that into a means of her livelihood. Pure milk is so difficult to find. All the milk would therefore be sold off readily. Karuna had to work the entire day but she was happy. What was visible on her face was not the shadow of disappointment or helplessness but the vigour of determination and courage. Every part of her body emitted an aura of self dignity. Her eyes reflect a divine light replete with unending gravity. All her afflictions: the grief of widowhood and the cruel blow of destiny—all that seems to have disappeared in the depths of that light.

She is ready to give her life for Prakash. Her happiness, her ambition her entire world even her heaven everything is sacrificed for Prakash; however it is not possible that Prakash makes some mischief and Karuna closes her eyes to that. She looks after his character very strictly. She is not just the mother of Prakash but his father too. In the adoration for her son, along with the mother's affection, father's sternness is also mixed. Her husband's last words still ring in her ears. That self elation that reflected on his face, that tint of self pride that had filled his eyes still keeps coming to her mind. Continuous reflection over her husband has made Aditya manifest himself in her eyes. She is forever conscious of his presence. She feels as if the soul of Aditya is always around to protect her. Her sole heartfelt desire is that after he grows up, Prakash follows on the footsteps of his father.

It was evening. A beggar woman had come to the doorstep asking for alms. Karuna was pouring water for the cows. Prakash was playing outside. He was a child after all! He thought of some mischief. He went inside and brought some crushed hay in a bowl. The beggar woman spread her begging sac in front of him. Prakash poured that crushed hay in the sac and ran clapping his hands loudly.

The beggar woman looked at it with fiery eyes and said, 'Oh lovable child! You have found only me to make a fool of! That is what your father and mother taught you? In that case surely you will make the name of your family shine.'

Hearing her voice Karuna came out and asked, 'What happened mother, whom are you talking to?'

The beggar pointed towards Prakash and said, 'He is your son, isn't it? See, he has dropped a bowl full of hay in my sac. I had a just a little bit of flour in my sac; now that too has got spoiled. Does one torment the poor like that? No one's days remains forever the way they are at present. Man should not become so conceited,'

Karuna called in a stern voice, 'Prakash?'

Prakash did not feel humiliated. He came with his head raised with pride and said, 'Why has she come to beg at our home? Why does she not do some job?'

'You don't feel ashamed; on the contrary you are getting angry,' Karuna said trying to make him understand.

'Why should I feel ashamed? Why does she come begging here every day? Here do we get anything for free?'

'If you did not want to give you could have told straightaway to go away. Why did you play that mischief?' said Karuna.

'How would she get rid of her habit otherwise?'

'Now you are going to get a thrashing from me,' said Karuna feeling annoyed.

'Why should I get a thrashing? You will beat me without a reason? In other countries, if someone begs he may be arrested. Not the other way round that beggars are encouraged.'

'How can one who is disabled work?'

'Than she should go and drown herself. Why does she remain alive?'

Karuna had no answer. She made the old woman depart after giving her some flour and lentil but this misguided logic of Prakash kept on gnawing her heart. Where did he learn this kind of superciliousness and impoliteness?'

Around mid night suddenly Prakash woke up. He saw the lantern was still alight and Karuna was weeping. He got up and said,

'Mother you didn't go to sleep?'

Karuna turned her face and said, 'I could not go to sleep. How did you get up? You are not feeling thirsty?'

'No mother, I don't know how I woke up—I did something really bad today.'

Karuna looked fondly at his face.

'I behaved very mischievously with that old woman. Forgive me, I will never to such a thing again,' said Prakash and started crying. Karuna embraced him with affection and kissing his cheek, she said, 'Son, are you saying that just to please me or you are really feeling regretful about it in your mind?'

'No mother,' said Prakash even as he sobbed, 'I am feeling really sorry in my heart. Next time when that old woman comes, I will give her a lot of money.'

Karuna heart was full of joy. She felt as if Aditya was standing there giving the child his blessing and saying, 'Karuna, don't feel sad, Prakash will bring glory to the name of his father. All your desires would be fulfilled.'

III

There was no correlation between Prakash's actions and his words and as days passed his character was becoming more pronounced. He was a thoughtful person indeed. He was getting a scholarship from the university and Karuna too was helping him to the extent possible; yet he would find it difficult to meet his expenses. He could give discourses on economising and simple living, yet his life style was not a bit different from the blind worshippers of latest fashions. He was obsessed forever with showing himself off.

There would forever a conflict between Prakash's heart and his mind. The mind would draw him towards the society but the heart towards his own self. The heart would forever overwhelm the mind. Before it the mind could not do anything. Social service is like cultivating an arid land, the greatest gift that one could get from there is name and fame and even that is not permanent; it is so ephemeral that one's entire earning of a life time may be lost in a moment. Therefore, his innermost thoughts would lean compulsorily towards a life full of comforts and luxury. It reached a point that that slowly he started hating the very idea of renunciation and self restraint. He considered scarcity and poverty as demeaning. He did not have a heart or feelings, he only had a mind. Is there a place for pain in the mind? It has place only for arguments and ideas.

There was flood in Sindh. Thousands of people were ruined. The university sent a relief committee there. A duel began in Prakash's mind: whether to go there or not. If he worked for his examinations for that much time he would get the first division. In the end he made an excuse of illness. Karuna wrote to him, 'I am sorry to hear that you did not go to Sindh. You could have gone there even if your were ill: after all there were doctors too in the committee!' Prakash did not reply to her letter.

There was a famine in Orissa. People started dying like flies. The Congress Party organized a relief mission for the suffering masses. Around that very time the university decided to send the students of History to visit Ceylon for a research project. Karuna wrote to Prakash, 'You must go to Orissa.' However Prakash was tempted to go to Lanka.

He remained in a state of indecision for many days. In the end Sri Lanka won over Orissa. This time Karuna did not write to him anything. She just kept crying.

After returning from Ceylon Prakash went home for the vacations. Karuna remained a little withdrawn from him. Prakash felt a bit ashamed and he resolved that whenever such an occasion comes next, he would surely make her mother feel happy. He returned to the university with that determination. But as soon as he reached there he got preoccupied with the examinations. But even after getting over with the examinations Prakash did not go home. One of the teachers in the college was going for a holiday to Kashmir. Prakash tagged along with him. When the result was declared and Prakash stood first, thought of home came to his mind! He immediately wrote a letter to Karuna and informed her about his arrival. To please his mother he also added a few sentences about social service and said that he was ready to abide with her orders and that he had decided to work in the field of education and that with that very idea in mind he had worked to attain this meritorious division. After all even our leaders respect the school teachers. Till now they have not got liberated from the attachment to these degrees. Even our leaders don't show so much respect to competence, enthusiasm and dedication as they show to degrees. Now they will respect me and offer me positions of responsibility, which earlier I could not get even if asked for them.

Karuna again had some hope.

IV

Soon after the college commenced Prakash received a letter from the Registrar. He informed Prakash about his getting a government scholarship for visiting England for further studies. Overcome with joy Prakash came to his mother, carrying the letter in his hand and said, 'Mother I have received a government scholarship for going to England for studies.'

'So what do you intend to do?' asked Karuna in an indifferent manner.

'What do I intend? Can anyone give up such an opportunity?'

'But you were planning to join as a volunteer.'

'You think, becoming a volunteer is the only way to serve the people? I can always become a volunteer after returning from England and mother, to tell you the truth, the amount of people's welfare a magistrate can do, even one thousand volunteers put together cannot hope to do. I am going to appear for the Civil Services examination and I am confident that I would succeed.'

'So you will be a magistrate?' asked Karuna feeling amazed.

'A magistrate having the intention to serve the people can do more for the welfare of people than one thousand senior workers of the Congress. There would be no eulogies for him in the newspaper, no one would clap at his discourses; throngs of people would not follow him in the processions and college students will not send him congratulatory letters but it is only a magistrate who can do render true service to the people.'

'But it is these very magistrates who mete out punishment to our social workers; it is they who order bullets to be fired on them,' Karuna said by way of raising an objection.

'If a magistrate harbours humanitarian feelings in heart then he can achieve the same end with softness that others cannot hope to do by even firing bullets.'

'I will not agree with that. The government does not give so much freedom to its officials. It merely lays down the policy and every government servant has to follow that. The first and foremost of government's policy is that it should become more entrenched and firm with each passing day. For that end it is essential to exterminate the idea of independence; if any magistrate works against this policy he would not last long as a magistrate. It was an Indian, who sentenced your father to three years of imprisonment for just a trifle. It was that very sentence, which took away his life; therefore my son, just obey this much of my request. Don't fall for these official positions. It would be acceptable to me if you eat frugally and dress frugally and render some service to the nation, rather than becoming an employee of the colonial government and live your life in luxury. Understand that the day you occupy such a chair your mindset will get transformed to that of a typical government servant. You would want that you get recognition among your seniors and that you get promotions. Take a crude example. Till the time a girl is unmarried she considers her parents' house as her home but the day she goes to her in-laws she starts considering her parental home as different from her own. Her father, mother, brothers all remain the same but that home is no more her own. That is the way of the world.'

'So you want simply that I should just keep facing the blows of adversities all my life' said Prakash feeling irritated.

'If by facing the blows of adversity you can retain the independence of your spirit then I would say it is better to face them.'

'So that is what you desire?' asked Prakash in a way as if he wanted to take a final decision.

'Yes, that I what I desire,' said Karuna in the same tone.

Prakash did not reply. He got up and went out and immediately and sent a letter of refusal to the Registrar, but from that very movement it was as if misfortune took over his very being. Apathetic and uninterested in anything he would keep lying around in his room. He would neither go out for a walk nor meet anyone. A month passed by. He did not have anymore that pink hue or brightness on his face; his eyes would appear as if they were like that of a beggar, full of supplication, his lips had forgotten their smile. It was as if all his liveliness, agility and simplicity had departed with that letter of refusal. Karuna understood his state of mind and she tried to make him forget his sorrow but the annoyed god would not get propitiated.

Finally, one day she said to Prakash, 'Son, if you are determined to go to England than you go. I would not tell you not to do so. I am sorry that I stopped you. If I had known it would affect you so much than I would not have come in your way. I stopped you with the sole intention that your father's soul would be pleased if he found you engaged in social service. That is the will he had made before he left this world.'

'How the hell can I go now. I have already refused the offer. They would not keep waiting for me till now. By now some other boy would have been selected. What else can I do? If it is your will that I should go around swallowing the dust of all the villages in the country side then let it be so.'

Karuna's pride was blown into smithereens. She intended to use her permission as an obstacle but she could not succeed. 'I don't think anyone would have been selected by now. Write to them that you are ready to go,'

'Nothing can be done now. People are only going to laugh. I have decided that I will mould my life according to your desire.'

'If you had made this resolution with a pure heart than you would not be living like this. You are carrying out your protest against me. If you fulfill my wishes suppressing your heart's desires, considering me like a thorn in your way, then what is the point? I would have appreciated if this desire had taken its origin in your heart on its own. Now you may as well write the letter to the Registrar.'

'I can't do that now.'

'So you will remain adamant and keep feeling sad like this?'

'I can't help it.'

Karuna did not say anything further. After a while Prakash noticed that she was going somewhere; however he did not say anything. It was not unusual for her to go out; but when the sun had set and Karuna did not return, Prakash started getting worried. Where did the mother go? This question came again and again to his mind. He kept sitting at the doorstep the entire night. All kinds of doubts arose in his mind. He recalled how sad Karuna was when she had left; how red were her eyes. Why could he not notice that at that time? Why had he become so blind thinking of his own self? Yes, now he remembered—she was wearing clean clothes and she had an umbrella in her hand. So has she gone somewhere far away? Whom should he ask? Apprehending that some calamity was going to take place he started crying.

It was a dark frightful night during the rainy season. Dark clouds were spread out in the sky like a scary dream. Prakash was looking towards the sky every now and then, as if Karuna was hidden there in the midst of those clouds. He decided that as soon as the morning broke he would set out with the search for his mother, but then suddenly someone knocked at the door. Prakash ran and opened the door and saw Karuna standing there. She looked so lost and her visage appeared so sad as if she had just got widowed, as if there was nothing left for her in the world, as if she was standing near a river watching her boat drowning and could not do anything about it.

'Mother where had you gone? You took a long time.'

'I had gone for some work. I got delayed,' she said looking towards the floor. Saying that she threw a sealed envelope before Prakash. He picked it up feeling inquisitive. It had the stamp of the university on it. He opened it immediately and read. A light flash of redness appeared on his face.

'Where did you find it, mother?' he asked.

I have brought it from your Registrar.

'Did you go there?'

'Yes what could I do?'

'But yesterday there was no train.'

'I engaged a motorcar.'

Prakash kept standing for a while and then said 'But when it is not really your wish, why are you sending me there?'

'It is because you have the desire to go there. I can't bear to see this sad state of yours. I have sacrificed twenty years of my life for your welfare; now I can not kill your greatest desire. I only wish that you are successful in your endeavours. That is my heartfelt desire.' said Karuna. Her throat got choked and she could not say anything more.

V

Prakash started preparing for his visit from that day itself. Whatever Karuna had was spent and she had to take even some loan. New suits were got stitched, suitcases were purchased. He was lost in his own world. He would be asking for something or the other every now and then. Karuna has become so frail in just one week, how grey her hair have started looking, how many wrinkles have surfaced on her face—he was oblivious to that all. In his eyes all that was visible were scenes of England. Ambition places a curtain on one's eyes.

The day of departure arrived. Today sunshine had manifested itself after many days. Karuna was taking out the old clothes of her husband. His coarse bed sheets, *kurtas* and pyjamas made of *khaddar*[44] were all still kept safely in the trunk. Every year they would be taken out and kept back after cleaning and dusting. Karuna took out those clothes again but today it was not for keeping them back after sunning them but for distributing them among the poor. She is angry with her husband today. That *lutiya*[45], clock and thread that were constant companions of Aditya and which she had worshipped for last twenty years were today thrown out in the courtyard; that cotton sac whose sling had always found its place on Aditya's shoulder was today thrown into the garbage; that picture in front of which she had been bowing during the last twenty years was today thrown mercilessly on the floor. She did not want to keep anything that would remind her of her husband in the house. Her inner self has become worn with sorrow and hopelessness. On whom else can she out her anger except for her husband? Who is there whom she can call her own? To whom can she narrate her sad story? Had he been alive would Prakash feel elated putting the chains of servitude around his neck? Who could make her understand that on such an occasion even Aditya could not have had done anything but to feel sorry.

Friends of Prakash had given him a farewell party. He had returned from there in the evening in a motorcar with some friends. After his travelling baggage had been kept in the car, he went inside and said to her mother, 'Mother, I am leaving now. I will write to you after reaching Bombay. Promise me that you will not cry and you will reply to my letters regularly.'

The way close relatives lose their equanimity when someone's dead body is taken out of the house Karuna too was in the same condition. Tears that had been withheld for long started flowing and waves of sadness start rising. There was a commotion in her heart, which shook every atom of her frail soul. She felt as if her foot had slipped in the water and she was being swept away by waves. No word of sadness or blessing came out of her mouth. Prakash touched her feet, his tears washing the feet of his mother and then he went out. Karuna stood there like a statue cast in stone.

Suddenly the milkman came and said, '*Bahuji, bhaiya*[46] has left. He was crying a lot.'

At that moment Karuna regained her consciousness. She noticed that there was no one around. A deathly silence prevailed in the house; it was as if her heart had stopped beating.

Suddenly Karuna looked upwards. She saw that Aditya was standing there with the dead body of Prakash in his hand. She fell down in a swoon.

VI

Karuna was alive, but she had no relation with the world anymore. Her small world that she had created in her imagination had gone into oblivion like a dream. Prakash, the bright light looking at which she had been living on in even the dark night of her life with a wealth of hopes in her heart had got extinguished and she had lost her everything. Now there was neither any refuge nor any need for it. Those cows whom she used to massage and feed both the times with her own hands would now keep staring towards the door with despair. There was no one now who would embrace and fondle the calves. There was no one for whom she needed to milk the cows and make butter milk. Who was there to be fed now? Karuna had now withdrawn her small world inside her own self.

However within a week Karuna's life changed its colour once again. Her miniscule world started swelling and attained global dimensions. That anchor that was keeping the boat tied to one place had come out. Now the boat will sail over the immense expanse of the ocean even though that enterprise might vanish in the immensity of the waves. She would now come and sit on her doorstep, gather all the children in the neighbourhood and make them drink milk. Then she would prepare all sorts of delicacies and feed the dogs. Now that had become her daily routine. Sparrows, dogs, cats, even the ants and insects all became her own. The door of her affection was not closed to anyone. In that little space that was only as big as a finger and which was not enough even for Prakash, now the entire world had found a place for itself.

One day a letter arrived from Prakash. Karuna threw it away. After a while she picked it up and tore and started feeding the sparrows; however when the evening fell, the pain in her heart revived—her heart became restless to read Prakash's letter. 'What does Prakash mean to me? What do I have to do with him? How does he matter to me? How is related to me?' she thought. 'Prakash is your everything, he is the souvenir of that immortal love of yours from which you have been deprived for ever. He is you life, he is the light of the lamp of your life, the sweetness of your unfulfilled desires, the swan who lives in the stream of your tears', replied her heart.

Karuna started gathering the pieces of that letter as if it was her own being that had got scattered. Each and every piece appeared to her as the footprint of her lost love. When all the pieces were gathered, Karuna sat in front of the lamp and started assembling them, as if a broken hearted man was trying to connect the broken strings of his love. Oh the love of a mother! The unfortunate woman spent the entire night trying to put together those pieces of paper. The letter was written on both the sides, so it was even more difficult to put the pieces in their correct place. Some word, some sentence in between would go missing. She would start looking for the missing piece. The whole night was spent but the letter was still incomplete.

It was daylight again. The young boys of the neighbourhood gathered with the desire for milk and butter, the dogs and the cats arrived, sparrows too started coming and jumping around in the courtyard, some sitting on the buttermilk churn, some on the platform where the *tulsi*[48] plant was kept; but Karuna had no time to spare to even lift her head.

It was afternoon, but Karuna had not lifted her head. She was neither hungry nor thirsty. Then the evening fell. The letter was still incomplete. The import of the letter could be made out—Prakash was going somewhere in a ship. His heart is troubled by something. But what was it that was troubling it, Karuna could not make out. She wanted to read each and every word that came out of the pen of her son and imprint it on her heart.

Three days passed like this. The evening had fallen. The eyes that had remained awake for three days winked for a while. Karuna saw a huge room in which there were tables and chairs laid out and in the middle on a high platform somebody is sitting. She saw carefully, it was Prakash.

In an instant a prisoner was brought in, his hands and legs were chained, his back bent; that was Aditya.

Karuna's woke up. Tears started flowing. She gathered all the pieces of the letter once and again and burnt them to ashes. There was nothing remaining except for a little bit of cinders which were tearing her heart away. In that small bit of ashes her doll-like childhood, her grief-stricken youth and her widowhood full of desires had all got submerged.

In the morning people found that the bird had flown out of its nest. A photograph of Aditya was still clinging to her empty heart resting there in the fond memory of her heartbroken husband and the ship of Prakash was sailing towards Europe.

A Goddess

Tuliya had not yet reached that phase of childlike shamelessness that people usually acquire in the old age, though her hair had turned white and her cheeks had fallen below her jaw line. She could not tell herself definitively what her age was, but according to people's estimation she had crossed a hundred years. Even now while walking she would cover her head and keep her eyes lowered as if she was a newly married girl.

Although she belonged to the community of hide makers but it would never so happen that she would feel tempted by some delicacy in anyone's house. There were many households of high caste people in the village. Tuliya frequented all of them. The entire village respected her and as for the housewives, they looked at her with reverence. They would insist that she visited their house; they would oil her hair and put *sindur*[48] in the parting of her hair. If there were any nice dish that was cooked like *halva* or *kheer* they would insist that she partook of it; however for the old woman what was more important was their respect than the taste of delicacies. She would never eat anything.

Tuliya had no one of her own. In her neighbourhood some people had fled from the village, some had fallen victim to plague and malaria and the few ruins that remained looked as if they were there beating their breasts remembering the parted ones. Only Tuliya's mud house remained. The journey of her life had reached that end where human beings get liberated from all bondages of society and religion. Now even the well to do people did not discriminate anymore with her on account of her caste—they were all ready to give her shelter in their houses. But why should the old woman with her self esteem should take the obligation of anyone? Why should she bring shame to the name of her husband whose face she had seen only once and that too about hundred years back? Yes just once!

When Tuliya got engaged she was merely five years old and her husband was an eighteen year old stalwart. After the marriage he had left for the East to earn her living. He thought it would take the young girl about ten to twelve years to come of age; therefore why should he not earn some money so that he could lead the life of a farmer without any care. However Tuliya became a young woman and then grew old but he never came home. For fifty years money orders keep arriving. Along with money orders, there would also be a letter with an address and it would be an order for thirty rupees. In the letter he would regularly tell her the woes of his helplessness, bondage and misfortune.

'What can I do Tula, I have great desire that I should come and live in our house with comfort in your company; however everything is in the hands of the destiny, we have no control over it. It is only when the God wishes that I would come. Be patient; as long as I am alive you would not have any discomfort. When I have got betrothed to you I would remain faithful to you till my last breath. What will happen when one is no more, who could know that?'

Usually all his letter would carry the same words and sentiments with a little bit of difference. Of course, in place of the flame of youth that used to be there in the letters written in his youth, all that remained was the ashes of despair. Nevertheless, for Tuliya all those letters were dear to her, as if they were fragments of her heart. She had never torn even one of them—can one tear such letter of good tidings—a small heap of them had got amassed. The colour of the pages had faded, even the ink had faded but for Tuliya they were still as full of life as full of curiosity as they were. They were all tied with a red thread and kept in a box like the savings of her marital bliss amassed over her brief life span. She would be full of joy when she received those letters. She would be full of pride and she would have them read to her many times over and keep crying again and again. That day she would make it a point to oil her hair and put vermillion in the parting of her hair, wear a colourful *sari* and touch the feet of her forbears and seek their blessings. Her marital bliss would get revived. For a village-woman living away from their husbands a letter is not something to be read and thrown away, it is like the life of her dear consort living faraway, dearer than her own body. Tuliya perhaps considered her husband's letters itself to be her husband. Had she seen any other form of her husband?

Young girls of the village would laugh and ask her, 'what aunty, can you remember the uncle, you must have *seen* him at least?' And then youthfulness would start gleaming on her face that was covered with creases and there would be redness in her eyes. With great joy she would say, 'how can I not remember him my child, his face is still there right before my eyes: a high forehead, big eyes, broad chest and a muscular body; nowadays there is hardly any such young man. He had teeth like pearls. He was wearing a red *kurta*. When we got married I asked him, 'will you get lot of ornaments made for him; otherwise I will not stay in your house.' I was young, my child, there was little shyness in me. After hearing what I said he laughed loudly and making me sit over his shoulders he said, "I will load you down with ornaments Tuliya, how many of them would you wear? I am going to a foreign land to make a fortune, I will send you money from there; you can then get lots of ornaments made for yourself. When I return, I too will bring a boxful of ornaments." My parents were not so rich they could afford to invite him with *barat*[49] to their house; so I got engaged at his house itself and in just one day he endeared to myself so much that when he was leaving I embraced him and started crying and said, "take me too along with you. I will cook your food, make your bed and wash your clothes". There were two three young boys of his age there. Right in front of them he smiled and said to me in my ear, "and you will not sleep with me?" So, I left him and stood away from him and throwing a pebble at him I said, "If you say foul words to me then I will tell you, yes!"'

From daily remembrance, this story of her life had become almost like the mantra of her life to be chanted every day. Her face would be worth seeing at such a moment. She would draw her veil and turn her face laughing away as if something like sorrow did not just exist in her life. She would narrate that sacred memory of her life and reflect the inner light of her inner self that had been protecting her from the thorns on the way of the journey of her life over a hundred years. What an everlasting desire it was that had not got faded by the harsh realities of her entire life!

II

There was a time when Tuliya was in the prime of her youth and young men would hover like insects around the lamp of her beauty, as if they were intoxicated. When she would tell the tales of their love, their frenzy and self surrender before her, in her trembling voice while her eyes would become moist then perhaps the souls of those martyrs would dance with joy in heaven if they heard Tuliya giving away in their name with both her hands what they could never get in their lives.

Her youth was blooming then. Wherever she would pass by the young men would hold their breath. Those days there was a *thakur*[32] by the name of Bansi Singh: very handsome and fun loving, the most gallant young man of the village, whose singing could be heard from a long distance in the silence of the night. He would make hundreds of rounds of Tuliya's house in a day. Whether it was by the side of the pond, fields or the village well or the barns, he would follow her like a shadow wherever she went. Sometimes he would come to her house carrying milk sometimes *ghee*[50]. He would say,

'Tuliya, I don't want anything from you, just accept whatever I bring to you as a gift. Don't speak with me if you don't want to, don't look at my face if you don't want to see it, but don't refuse my offerings. I would be happy merely with that.'

Tuliya was not such a simpleton; she knew that it was just a way to latch on to her but she did not realise how she was caught in his deceptions— no it was not getting caught in deception but it was because she had pity on his youth. One day he had brought a basket of ripe grafted mangos! She had never eaten a grafted mango. She took the basket from him. Thereafter every day baskets of mangos started arriving. One day when Tuliya was going inside her house with the basket of mangos, Bansi slowly caught her hand and kept it on his breast and then immediately fell over to his feet. He then said,

'Tuliya, if you don't have pity over me even now then just you kill me today. That I get killed by your hands that is my sole desire.'

Tuliya threw the basket and getting her feet released she stepped back a little and looking at him with eyes full of rage, she said,

'Okay Thakur, now you just go away from here, otherwise either you or I won't remain here. Let your mangos be consigned to flames, what else I can tell you! My man is staying in some godforsaken foreign land for *this* reason that here I cheat on him behind his back! He is a man, he earns lot of money; can he not keep some other woman? Is there a dearth of women in the world? Will you read the letters that he sends in my name? Whatever state he might be in, can I see that sitting here, but he sends me money regularly. Why? So that I have fun here with others! As long as he thinks that I belong to him and he belongs to me, Tuliya will remain faithful to him, both by heart as well as deeds. When I got married to him I was a five years old innocent girl. What enjoyment did he derive with me? He is remaining faithful merely to the act of holding my hand. When he can live up to his love even though he is a man, then shall I cheat on him even though I am a woman?'

Saying that she went inside and threw the box full of letters before the Thakur. But Thakur's eyes seemed to be sealed and his lips were getting contracted. It seemed as if he was sinking in the earth. After a while he folded his hands and said, 'I committed a big offense Tuliya. I did not understand you. Now the only punishment for me is that you kill me this very moment. That is the only way to redeem a sinner like me.'

Tuliya did not take pity on him. She thought he was still playing tricks. In an irritated voice she said, 'If you feel like dying then die. Are there no wells or ponds on this earth? Don't you have some sword or dagger? Why should I kill someone?'

Thakur looked at him with desperation, 'So that is your order.'

'How can that be my order? Those who want to die don't ask for orders from anyone.'

Thakur went away and the next day his corpse was found floating in the river. People thought that he must have gone there to bathe early in the morning and his feet might have slipped. For months there were discussions on this topic in the village but Tuliya did not open her mouth; she stopped going there.

Soon after the death of Bansi Singh his younger brother took hold of all the estate and started tormenting his widow and the child. The sister in law would taunt him and he would charge her of misdeeds. Finally the poor widow got sick of her life and left the home. The entire village seemed to be asleep. Tuliya had had her dinner and with a lantern in hand she came out to feed the cow. In the light she noticed the *thakurain*[51] walking away with silent steps. She was sighing and cleaning her eyes with the border of her sari. The three year infant was in her arms.

'Where are you going so late in the night *thakurain*? Listen, what is the matter, why are you crying?' asked Tuliya.

Thakurain had left the home but she did not know herself where she was going. She looked at Tuliya with moist eyes and moved forward without replying. How could she reply? Her throat was choking with tears which at that time had surged even more.

Tuliya came and stood before her, 'I will not let you go even one step further till you don't tell me.'

Thakurain stopped and filling with rage her eyes that were full of tears she said, 'What will you get by asking me? How does it matter to you?'

'It does not concern me? Do I not live in your village? If people in the village do not help each other in each other's misery, then who else would?'

'In this world who is there who helps anyone Tuliya? When the people in my own house did not support me and just after the death of your brother became thirsty for my blood then from whom else can I hope for anything? The state of our household is not hidden from you. There is no place for me there now. My brother in law and his wife, for whom I used to be ready to give my life, have now become my enemy. They wish that I just keep lying in a corner like an orphan eating just one *roti*. I am not a keep of anyone, I am a married woman. I came here after getting married in front of ten villages. I will not let go of my estate and I will not rest in peace till I get back my share.'

'Your brother', those two words sounded so dear to Tuliya that she embraced the *thakurain* and holding her hand she said, 'So sister, come and stay in my house. Someone else may help you or not but Tuliya will be with you till her last breath. My house is not worthy of you but if nothing else at least there is peace there and however base I may be by birth, I am at least your sister.'

Thakurain's astonished eyes were focused on Tuliya's face.

'I don't want that because of me my brother in law becomes your enemy too.'

'I am not afraid of enemies; otherwise I would not be staying here all alone in this habitation.'

'But I don't want that any trouble comes on you because of me.'

'Who is going to tell him, and who will come to know that you are inside.'

Thakurain felt reassured. Hesitatingly she came inside with Tuliya. Her heart was feeling heavy. She who was the mistress of a big solidly built house was now seeking refuge in that hut.'

There was only one cot in the house. *Thakurain* and her child slept on that while Tuliya stretched herself on the floor. There was just one blanket with which the *thakurain* covered herself. Tuliya would cover herself with a piece of carpet and pass the night. How to welcome the guest, how to keep her comfortable, that is what she would keep thinking. Washing *thakurain's* utensils, arranging her clothes, feeding the child, all these tasks she would attend to with such enthusiasm as if she was worshipping the goddess. *Thakurain* was a *thakurain* even in her adversity: proud, pleasure loving and without imagination. She would live as if it was her own house and she would boss over Tuliya as if she were her servant. However Tuliya was living up to the love of her unfortunate lover towards her. She would never take anything to heart and there would be not one crease on her forehead.

One day the *thakurain* said, 'Tula, you look after the child, I will go out for a few days. This way I will just remain here all my life eating your bread, but how will the fire in my heart get extinguished? This shameless brother in law does not have any feeling about where his sister in law has gone. In his heart he must be happy that the thorn in his path has been removed. As soon as he comes to know that I have not gone to my parents and living somewhere else, he would immediately malign me and the whole society will support him. Now I should start worrying about myself.'

'Where do you want to go sister? If you don't mind shall I too come along with you? Where will you go all alone?' asked Tuliya.

'I will look for some stick with which to crush that snake."

Tuliya could not understand her intent. She stared at her face.

Thakurain said with shamelessness, 'you don't even understand this much! You want me to put it bluntly? What other weapon does a helpless woman have to safeguard herself except for her beauty? Now I will take recourse to that very weapon. You know what would be the price of this beauty? The head of this wolf! Whoever is the head of this *pargana*[52] will now fall under the sway of my magic. Where is the man who can save himself from the magic of a young woman, even if he were a saint? If I lose my soul in the process, I don't care. I can't bear that I go around in the forests feeding on leaves whereas that villain lords there twirling his moustache.'

Tuliya came to learn how deep a blow the heart of that proud woman had received, to alleviate the pain of which she is ready to play not only on her life but her honour itself which she considers even dearer than her life. The image of Bansi Singh pleading before her came before her eyes. He was a strong man; with his immense strength he could have easily used force on Tuliya. Who was there in the silence of the night that could have rescued the poor helpless woman? But how that chastisement given by a devout woman had won over Bansi Singh; it was as if a dreadful black snake had got charmed by a melodious song. Today the family honour of that truthful brave man is in danger. Will Tuliya allow the name of his family to be disgraced and not do anything? Never! If Bansi Singh had considered her to be dearer than his life then she too would safeguard his honour putting at sake her own honour.

'Don't go anywhere sister for the time being; allow me first to test my powers. Even if I lose my honour no one would care anything about it. As for you, behind your honour it is the honour of your entire family that would be at stake.'

Thakurain smiled as she looked at her and said, 'What do you know about this art Tuliya?'

'Which art?'

'The same about making a fool of the menfolk.'

'I am a woman.'

'But you know nothing about the character of the men.'

'That is what both of us had learnt in the womb of our mothers.'

'Tell me what you would do.'

'Same as what you were going to do. You wanted to try your magic on the administrator of this area; I will cast my net on your brother in law.'

'He is a very shrewd man.'

'That's exactly what is to be seen.'

III

Tuliya spent the rest of the night in making the plan and thinking over how to execute it. Like a competent general she made a plan of attack in her mind. She was sure of her victory. The enemy was unwary; he had no clue about the attack.'

Bansi Singh's younger brother Girdhar was walking past with his usual swagger carrying a thick six feet long stick when Tuliya called to him, 'Thakur, please keep this bundle of hay on my head. I am unable to pick it up.'

It was after noon. Labourers had gone back from the field. Egrets had started getting up. Tuliya was standing near a tree with a big load of hay in front of her. Sweat was trickling down her forehead.

Thakur got startled and looked towards Tuliya and at that very moment the edge of her sari that was covering her breast slipped down and the red blouse under it became visible. She immediately covered herself but in that hurry the string of flowers braided in her hair flashed like lightening in his eyes. Girdhar's heart became unsteady. In his eyes there was a trace of intoxication and a flash of redness and a faint smile on his face.

He had seen Tuliya thousands of time with hungry covetous eyes, but full of pride for her beauty and truthfulness Tuliya would never even raise her eyes towards him. There would be such dryness and indifference in her mannerism that Thakur's courage would fail and his entire interest in her would be reduced to naught. Of what avail could be a net or grains when it concerns a bird that is flying in the sky. But today the same bird had come and perched on a branch before him and it appeared that it was hungry. So why should he not hurry with the grain and the net.

Feeling elated he said, 'I'll carry it Tuliya, why should you pick it up on your head.'

'And if someone sees it he will wonder what has gone wrong with the Thakur.'

'I don't care for the barking of dog.'

'But I do.'

Thakur did not give up. He picked up the bale of hay and placing it on his head he started walking feeling so great as if he was carrying the treasure of the entire world.

IV

One month passed by. Tuliya had cast her spell on the Thakur and now she was making him play like a fish. Sometimes she would ease the bait a little sometimes tighten it. Thakur had gone out hunting but had got trapped himself. Even after sacrificing his conscience, values and reputation he had not been able to get the boon from the goddess. Tuliya was as distant from him as ever.

One day he said to Tuliya, 'how long will you make me pine like this? Let's run away somewhere.'

Tuliya tightened the noose even more, 'Yes why not! And when you turn away from me I would be left in a lurch: I will lose my hearth as well as home'.

'You don't have faith on me even now?' said Thakur in a complaining voice.

'The bee collects the nectar and flies away.'

'And doesn't the moth get burnt and reduced to ash?'

'How do I believe in you?'

'Have I ever refused to carry out your order?'

'You must be thinking that you will be able to hook Tuliya merely by offering her a colourful sari and a few ornaments. I am not as simple as that.'

Tuliya had fathomed what was in Thakur's heart. Thakur looked at her with astonishment.

'When a man leaves his house he makes some arrangement to live somewhere in advance,' said Tuliya.

'Come and stay with me like the mistress of my house. How many times I have told you that,' said Thakur feeling happy.

'Today I live like the mistress of the house and tomorrow it may happen that I may not remain even as a keep, isn't it?' said Tuliya goggling her eyes.

'Do what your heart tells you to do. As for me I am your slave.'

'You give me your word?'

'Yes I do. Not once but hundred time, thousand times.'

'You will not go back on your word?'

'Giving your word and not keeping it the job only of unmanly persons.'

'Then you transfer half of your estate in my name.'

Thakur was ready to offer her feet a room in his house, five or ten *bighas*[27] of land, clothes and ornaments but he did not dare to transfer half of his estate. If tomorrow she gets annoyed with him over something, then half of his fortune will be lost to him. How can one have faith on such a woman! He could never imagine that Tuliya would take such a tough test of his love. He felt angry with her.

'This daughter of a hide maker, she thinks she is a fairy just because she is a little good looking.'

His love was limited to the allure of her beauty. That love which makes one ready to sacrifice oneself and considers that sacrifice in itself to be the success of life was not there in him.

'I didn't know you love my estate not me' he said.

Tuliya replied immediately, 'As if I didn't know that you love only my beauty and my youth and not me.'

'You consider love as a trade off in the market place.'

'Yes I do. For you love would be like the moon that shines and lasts for a few days; for me it would only be the darkness thereafter. When I am giving my everything to you I also want to take something in return. If you really loved me you would be ready to transfer your entire estate in my name not just half of it. Am I going to carry your estate somewhere on my head? But it is good that I came to know your mind. God forbid such a time comes—after all no one has a good time forever—but if ever such a time comes that you have to ask me for a favour, then Tuliya would show you how generous the heart of a woman could be.'

Tuliya went off feeling irritated but she was neither despairing nor disappointed. Whatever had happened was a part of the scheme that she had thought of. What was going to happen next, she did not have any doubts about.

V

Thakur had saved his estate but at a very high price. His heart was forever feeling discontented. It was as if nothing remained in his life any more. His estate was before his eyes but Tuliya was inside her heart. When Tuliya came everyday in front of him and with her arched eyes shot an arrow in his heart, she was real. Now the Tuliya which was forever in her heart was like a dream that is more addictive, more bewitching than reality.

Tuliya is visible sometimes like a flash as if in a dream and then like a dream itself she vanishes. Girdhar would be looking for an occasion to tell her about the pain that afflicted his heart but Tuliya would keep away even from his shadow. Girdhar was now realizing that even though his estate was necessary to make his life happy, Tuliya was far more important than that. He would feel angry for his miserliness. How does it matter if the estate was in his name or in Tuliya's. What is there in such a small thing? Tuliya was insisting on it because she was worried that if I am not faithful to her then she may be rendered almost an orphan. When I am her slave without her asking anything in return then how could I be unfaithful to her? Would I be unfaithful to her for whose one glance, one word I keep on pining? If he had met her somewhere all alone he would have told her,

'Tula whatever I have is yours. If you ask I will make a deed, I will make any deed you like. Whatever offence I have caused to you I am sorry for that. The attachment that one has for one's land made me say those words. It was that very conventional greed that had come between you and me. But now I have realized that in this world only that thing has the maximum value which gives you happiness and love. If one finds happiness in penury then that is the most important thing for which a man would sacrifice his land and ownership. Even today there are so many who have kicked off the comforts of life and are happy roaming around in the forests and mountains. And I did not understand even such a small thing. Oh, my misfortune.'

VI

One day Tuliya sent Thakur a message: 'I am ill, come and look me up, who knows whether I will even survive or not.'

Thakur had not seen Tuliya for so many days. He had even made rounds of her doorstep on numerous occasions but she could not be seen. Now when he got this message it was as if he had fallen from a hill. It was about ten in the night. He had not even heard the full message before he ran off. His heart was beating and his head was swaying. 'Tuliya is ill! What will happen now? O God! Why don't you make me ill? I am ready to even die in place of her. The dark trees on both the sides looked like the messengers of the god of death running along with him. Every now and then he could hear inside his mind a voice, submerged in desire and pain, 'Tuliya is ill.'

'His Tuliya has called for him. Called that treacherous, idiotic, lowly murderer to come and look her up, for who knows whether she would survive or not. If you don't survive then I too will not remain alive, oh yes, I will not survive! I will hit my head against the wall and die. Then you as well as I would be consigned to the flames on the same pyre, our dead bodies would be taken away at the same time.'

He hastened his steps. Today he would place his everything at the feet of Tuliya. She considers that he is not faithful. Today he would show her what is being faithful. If he is not faithful in this life then he will be after his death. Whatever he could not do in these few days of his life time he would keep performing for eons to come. His love would become a ballad that will be sung in each and every household.

There was some doubt in his mind, whether he would be able to give up the attachment for his life? He beat his breast loudly and said aloud, 'for what the longing for this life? And after all the life too is she only who is ill. Let me see how death can take away my life and leaves my dead body behind.

With a beating heart and trembling steps he entered Tuliya's house. She was lying there on her cot covered by a bed sheet and in the light emitted by the lantern her yellowing face appeared as if it was resting in the lap of death.

He laid his head at her feet and said in a voice drowned by tears, 'Tula, this unfortunate wretch is lying at your feet. Won't you open your eyes?'

Tuliya opened her eyes and casting a compassionate glance towards him she said in a painful voice,

'Is that you Girdhar Singh? You have arrived? Now I will die in peace. My heart was very anxious to see you once. Please forgive me for whatever I said to you and don't cry for me. What is there in this body which is made of dust, Girdhar! It will go back to dust. But I will never leave your company. I will remain with you forever like your shadow. You will not be able to see me, you will not be able to talk to me but Tuliya would remain with your twenty four hours whether you are awake or asleep. Don't disgrace yourself for me Girdhar! Let not my name come ever be uttered by you. Yes, sprinkle a few drops of water on the cinders of my pyre. That will calm down the flames of my heart.'

Girdhar was crying profusely. If I had a dagger with me I would have stabbed my heart with it right now and given my life right in front of her.

Tuliya said after a while, 'I will not survive Girdhar, I will make you a request, will you agree?'

Girdhar beat his breast and said, 'My dead body too will be taken out from here along with yours Tuliya. What will I do if I remain alive now and how do I live now even if I have to? You are my life, O Tuliya.'

He felt as if Tuliya had smiled.

'No, no don't do such something immature like that. You too have children; you have to bring them up. If you really love me truly then don't do anything that will make anyone even get any scent of this love. Don't bring a bad name to your Tuliya after her death.'

'As you desire' said Girdhar crying.

'I have only one request to make to you.'

'Now I will live only for the purpose that I fulfill your order, that alone will be the aim of my life.'

'I only request that you keep your sister in law with the same respect and dignity as she enjoyed with Bansi Singh. Give her half share to her.'

'But my sister in law is with her parents now and she said she will never come back.'

'That was something really bad you did Girdhar, really bad. Now I realize why I used to get such bad dreams every day. If you want that I should recover, then prepare the documents as soon as you can and leave the deed here with me. It is this very mercilessness of yours that is costing me my life. Now I have realised why Bansi Singh used to come again and again in my dreams. I have no other malady. It is only Bansi Singh who is tormenting me, now you just go. If you delay than you will not find me alive. For the injustice done by you Bansi Singh is punishing me.

'But where can I get the papers made in the night? Where will I find the stamp paper now, who will write it, where are the witnesses.' Girdhar said in a subdued voice.

If you do the paperwork by tomorrow evening my life will be saved Girdhar. Bansi Singh is after me, it is he who is torturing me because he knows that you love me. It is only because of your love that I am losing my life. If you delay than you will not find Tuliya alive.'

'I will go right away Tuliya. Your wish is my command. Had you told me this earlier then why would you reach such a state? I hope it does not so happen that I am not able to see you and my heart's desire remains buried therein.'

'No, no I won't die till tomorrow evening, believe me.'

Girdhar left then and there and covered a distance of twenty five miles over the night. He reached the town by day break and consulted the lawyers, purchased the stamp paper and willed half his estate in the name of his sister in law and got it registered and by the time of lighting of lamps in the evening, feeling tired, harassed, hungry, thirsty and trembling as he was caught between hope and despair, he came and stood in front of Tuliya. It was ten in the night. Those days there were neither any train nor buses, so the poor fellow had to cover the arduous journey of fifty miles on foot. He was so tired that every step felt to him like climbing a mountain. But he was afraid lest something unfortunate happens.

'You have come back Girdhar? Is it done?' Tuliya asked with her heart full of happiness.

Girdhar placed the deed in front of her and said, 'Yes Tula I have done that but if you don't get well than my life too would go along with yours. Whether the people laugh over it or cry, I don't care. You can ask me to swear if I had even a gulp of water to drink.'

Tuliya got up and keeping the papers under her pillow she said,

'Now I am feeling very well. I will be absolutely all right by tomorrow morning. I will not forget this kind deed that you have done for me till my death. But right now I had had a nap. I saw in my dream that Bansi Singh was standing near my bed and saying, "Tuliya you are a married woman, your husband is sitting far away remembering your name. If he wanted he would have taken another woman but he is relies on you and will remain like that all his life. If you betray him then I will turn your enemy and then I will not rest till I have taken your life. If you care for your welfare than stick to your piousness. If you play foul with him I will take your life the same day." Saying just that much and glaring at me with his red and angry eyes he went away.'

Gidhar looked for a moment toward the face of Tuliya on which a divine aura of a goddess seemed to prevail. All of a sudden it was as if a curtain was removed from his eyes and he could understand the whole conspiracy. He kissed the feet of Tuliya with true reverence and said, 'I have understood all Tuliya, you are a goddess.'

A Winter Night

Halku came and told his wife, 'The bailiff has come. Give me the money that is lying at home; let me give it to him so that I get rid of him.'

Munni was sweeping the floor with a broom. She turned back and said, 'There are just three rupees, if you give them how will we buy a blanket? How are we going to spend the winter during the months of *Magh*[53] and *Pous*? Tell him we will pay him at the time of the harvest, not now.'

Halku stood there for a moment in a state of indecision. Winter was round the corner. Without a blanket he would not be able to sleep in the fields during the night. But the bailiff would not agree, he will threaten and abuse. I don't care if I die of cold in winter, at least this trouble will be averted. Thinking thus, carrying his huge bulk, Halku, whose name belied his built [54,] approached his wife and flattering her he said,

'Come on give; let me get my neck free from him. As for blanket, I will think of some other solution,'

Munni withdrew from him and arching her eyes, she said, 'You will find surely some solution! Let me also hear what solution you will find? Will someone give you the blanket in charity? God knows how much there remains to be paid; it does not seem to come to an end. I say why don't you give up farming? You keep toiling till you are almost dead and when it is the time to harvest then you pay them their dues and that's the end of it. As if we have taken birth only to pay the dues. You keep toiling for your stomach only. God save us from such farming. I will not give the money, not at all.'

'So shall I listen to his insults?' Halku said feeling sad.

'Why should he insult, is he the ruler here?' But even as she said that her arched eyebrow became a little relaxed. There was a harsh reality in what Halku had said; it was staring at her as if some monstrous animal was staring at her.

She went and took the money out from the alcove and bringing them to Halku handed them over to him. Then she said, 'You leave this tilling of land. If you work as a labourer you will at least be able to eat one meal happily. At least no one will be able to bully you. Of what use this cultivation! You keep on slogging and then whatever you get you put it back in it, and on top of that this oppression.'

Halku took the money and went out in a manner as if he was going to take out his heart and give it to someone. He had saved each penny out of the proceeds of his hard work to amass those three rupees to buy a blanket. They were being taken away from him today. With every step his poor forehead was getting bent by the weight of his poverty.

II

It was a dark night in the month of *Pous*. The stars in the sky also seemed to be shivering. At the edge of his field, Halku was sitting on a small cot made of bamboos under an umbrella of sugarcane leaves, covering himself with his old thick bed sheet. Under the cot his companion dog Zabra was curled up against his stomach and making sounds of *kun kun* because of the cold. Neither of them was able to go to sleep. Halku touched his knees with his neck and said, 'Why Zabra, are you feeling cold? I was telling you to lie down on the hay at the house; what did you come here for? Now suffer this cold, what can I do? You thought I came here to feast on *halwa* and *poouri* and so you came running in front of me. Now keep crying in the name of your grandmother.'

Zabra wagged his tail lying on his belly and kept on making the sound of *kun kun*.

'Don't come with me from tomorrow otherwise you will freeze. This whore of a westerly wind is bringing icy cold from god knows where. Let me get up and make a *chillum*. Let at least the night get over somehow. I have had eight *chillums*. This is the fun of being a cultivator! And there are those near whom even if the cold ventures to go it would run back frightened by the heat. With all their thick mattresses, quilts and blankets dare the cold go near them? Destiny is great. It is we who keep toiling and the others have all the fun.

Halku got up and taking out a little bit of fire from the ditch, in which some cow dung cakes were smouldering, he filled his *chillum*. Zabra also got up.

Smoking the chillum Halku said, 'You want to smoke the chillum, it is not as if it would drive away the cold, though of course it diverts your mind.'

Zabra looked at his face with his eyes that were overflowing with love.

'Just bear this cold tonight. From tomorrow I will spread some hay here. You may sit covering yourself with it; you will not feel cold.'

Zabra placed his paws on Halku's knees and brought its mouth near his. Halku could feel his warm breath.

Halku lay down once again after finishing the chillum telling himself that he would sleep for a while this time, come what may; but within seconds he started shivering. He would turn one side and then turn the other side but the cold was weighing down on his chest like a ghost.

When he could not bear it anymore, he woke up Zabra lightly and patting on his head made him sleep in his lap. There was a foul odour emanating from the body of the dog but hugging it in his lap he was deriving such a comfort that he had not got for months. Zabra was thinking that it was heaven itself there and in the pious soul of Halku there was not even the slightest feeling of aversion towards that dog. He would have embraced even a close friend or a brother with the same ardour. He was not feeling injured by his poverty that had driven him to that state. No, it was as if this inimitable friendship had opened all the doors of his soul and each of its atoms was reflecting a bright light.

Suddenly Zabra sensed the movement of some animal. This extraordinary intimacy had given birth to a new strength which considered the gusts of icy wind as nothing. It leapt and came out of the umbrella and started barking. Halku called him many times lovingly, but it would not come near him. It kept on running around and barking. Even if it would return for awhile, it would soon run away immediately. Sense of duty seemed to be bouncing in his heart like desires.

III

One more hour passed by. The night had started intensifying the cold with a wind. Halku got up and touching both his knees with his chest he hid his head inside it; even then the cold did not seem to reduce. He felt as if his entire blood had frozen and instead of blood it was ice flowing in his veins. He bowed down and looked toward the sky to make out how much of the night still remained. The seven stars were not even half way up in the sky. It is only when they come up then it would be morning. Right now many hours still remained of the night.

At a small distance from Halku's field there was a mango orchard. The autumn had commenced. There were heaps of leaves lying in the orchard. Halku thought of going there to gather some leaves so that he could burn them and derive some warmth. If someone sees me gathering the leaves in the night he would think I am a ghost. Who know, some animal may be hiding there but now I cannot bear to sit anymore like this.

He went to a nearby *arhar* field and plucked out some plants and making a broom out of them and taking a smoldering cow dung cake along with him he headed towards the orchard. Zabra saw him coming and came near and started wagging its tail.

I can't bear it anymore Zabru. Let's go and gather some leaves and make a fire to warm ourselves. Once we feel a little warm, then we can come back and sleep. There still remains many hours of night.

Zabra expressed its willingness making sound of *kun, kun* and headed towards the orchard.

An intense darkness prevailed in the orchard and the heartless wind blew in the dark trampling the leaves. Drops of dew were falling drop by drop from the trees.

Suddenly there was a draft of wind which brought with it a whiff of the henna flowers.

What a nice fragrance it was, Zabru. Are you too getting the perfume in your nose?

Zabra had found a bone lying on the ground. He was chewing on it.

Halku kept the fire on the ground and started collecting the leaves. In a short while a big heap of leaves got amassed. His hands were feeling frozen and his bare feet were feeling numb and he was making a hill of leaves. He would burn to ashes the cold in this fire.

In a short while the bonfire started. Its upper flames were leaping and touching the leaves of the tree above. In that unsteady glow the huge trees in the orchard looked as if they were carrying an immense darkness on the top of their heads. In that limitless sea of darkness that glow seemed to be like an unsteadily moving boat.

Halku was sitting in front of the fire basking in its heat. A little later he took away the sheet that covered him and kept it under his armpit and spread both his legs as if he was challenging the cold. Conquering the immense might of the cold he was not able to hide the pride of his victory in his heart.

'What Zabbar, you are not feeling cold now?' He asked Zabra.

Zabra wagged its tail.

'Come on let's jump and cross over the fire. Let's see who is able to do it. If you get burnt I am not going to get you cured.'

Zabbar looked keenly towards the fire.

'Don't tell Munni, otherwise she will fight with me.'

Saying that he jumped and crossed over that fire. The flames touched his feet a little but that was nothing. Zabra went around the fire and then stood near him.

'Come on not this way, you have to jump over the fire and come here. He jumped again and reached the other side of the fire.'

IV

The leaves had burnt out. There was darkness once again in the orchard. A little bit of fire still remained under the cinders that would lit up whenever there was a gust of wind and close its eyes in a moment soon thereafter.

Halku covered himself once again with the sheet and started humming a song sitting near the hot ashes. His body had regained the warmth but as the cold increased he was getting overpowered with laziness.

Zabra barked aloud and ran towards the field. Halku sensed as if a band of animals had entered his field. It was perhaps a pack of *nilgais*[55]. He could hear clearly the sound of their running and jumping around. He then felt as if they were grazing in his field. He could hear clearly the sound of their chewing.

'No one can enter the field as long as Zabra is there,' he said to himself, 'he is going to bite them. It is perhaps my imagination. Where is it now? I can't hear anything now. What a deception I had felt.'

'Zabra, Zabra' he shouted out aloud.

Zabra kept on barking. It did not come back near him.

He could hear again the sound of grazing. This time he could not deceive himself. He detested the idea of moving from his place. How comfortably he had been sitting. To go to the field in this bitter cold and run after animals seemed unbearable. He did not move from his place.

Sitting where he was he shouted, 'move, move, move!'

Zabra barked again. The animals were chewing away the crop which was ready. What a nice crop it was but these villainous animals are going to destroy it.

Halku got up with a firm determination and walked a few steps but there was such a cold gust of wind that bit him like a scorpion that he came and sat near the dying fire and started warming himself raking the cinders.

Zabra was barking on the top of its voice, the *nilgais* were chewing away on the crop and Halku was sitting peacefully near the warm ashes. A sense of inactivity seemed to be holding him from all around like ropes tightening around him.

He lay down next to the ashes on the warm ground and went to sleep covering himself with his sheet.

When he got up in the morning it was sunshine all around and Munni was saying, 'Now will you just keep on sleeping today. You came and settled down here and there the entire field has been devastated.'

Without getting up Halku asked, 'Are you coming from the field?'

'Yes the entire crop has been devoured. Now, does anyone sleep like this! Of what use your coming and sitting on guard here?'

'Here I barely escaped death and you are talking about the crop. I had such a severe stomach ache, such an ache that I alone know,' Halku made an excuse.

Both of them came near the boundary of the field. They saw the entire field was trampelled over and Zabra lying stretched out as if he was dead.

Both of them were looking at the state of the field. Munni's face was overshadowed with sadness but Halku was happy.

'Now we are going to have to make do by working as labourers.'

'At least one will not have to sleep here in this cold during the night,' said Halku with a happy face.

The Thakur's Well

As Zokhu put his mouth to his *lota*[45] he got a strong stench.

'What kind of water is this?' he asked Gangi looking at that round water pot 'I can't make myself drink it because of the foul smell. My throat is drying and you are giving me this stinking water to drink.'

Gangi used to fill water every evening. The well was far away; it was difficult to go there again and again. There was no smell in the water that she had fetched yesterday; how is it that smells today. When she touched her nose to the pot, she found it had a foul smell indeed.

'Some animal must have fallen inside the well and died; but from where will she get other water now? Who will let her climb the Thakur's well? People will scold her from afar. Sahuji's well is on the other side of the village but who will let her fill water even there? There is no third well in the village', thought Gangi.

Zokhu has been ill since many days. He kept lying there enduring the thirst for some time after which he said, 'I can't remain without water any more now. Give, I will hold my nose and drink a little.'

Gangi did not give her the water. She knew that the sickness would only increase by bad water. She did not know that merely by boiling the water its impurities go away.

'How will you drink this water? God knows which animal it was that died. I will get some water from the other well.'

'From which well will you get water' Zokhu said looking towards her looking astonished.

'Thakur and Sahu both have wells. Will they not let me fill even one pot?'

'You will get your hands or legs broken and nothing else. Just sit here quietly. Thakur will hit you with a stick; Sahuji will charge you five times for one. Who understands the pain of the poor folks like us? Even if we die no one comes to our doorstep even to peep inside, leave aside helping carry your coffin. Would these kind of people allow you to fill water from their well?'

There was bitter truth in those words. What could Gangi say, but she did not let him drink the smelling water.

II

It was nine o'clock in the night. The tired and worn out labourers had gone to sleep. In front of Thakur's door some there was a gathering of five or ten people engaged in some conversation, who looked as if they had no care or worries left in life. The days of bravery in the battle field had gone by. The conversation in progress was about legal bravery.

'How astutely the Thakur bribed the police inspector in a particular case and came out clean. How intelligently he was able to get a copy of a famous court decision. The legal officer as well as his subordinates used to say that the copy could not be given. Someone asked for fifty, the other for hundred. Here he managed to slip out the copy without paying a penny. You have to know how to get the work done.'

At that very time Gangi reached the well to get some water.

A weak glow from the wick of the lamp was reaching up to the well. Gangi sat behind the platform waiting for the occasion. The entire village drinks water from this well. There is no interdiction for any of them; it is these unfortunates who could not fill water there.

Gangi's revolting mind started making attacks on customary restrictions and compulsions—'why are we people lower and why are they high? Is it because they wear a thread around their neck?[57] Each one of them here is a past master. They rob, they do frauds and trickery, they file false suits. Now the other day, this very *Thakur* stole the sheep of that shepherd and later on killed it and ate it up. It is these very pundits in whose household gambling goes on all the year round. It is this very Sahuji who sells *ghee* adulterated with oil. They make you work and when it comes to paying wages it is as if their maternal grandmother is going to die[58]. In which way are they higher than us; we don't go around shouting in the streets that we are high. If I come to the village sometime, then they look at me with such covetous eyes. They look so envious; yet they feel proud that they are higher than others.'

There was a sound of someone coming to the well. Gangi's heart started beating. If someone sees me it would be a disaster. She picked up her *ghada*[58] and the rope and walked off bending forward and stood in the dark shadow of a tree. 'Do these people ever take pity on anyone? They thrashed the poor Mehngu so much that he kept on spitting blood for months—merely because he refused to work for them without any wages. It is on top of this that these people claim that they are higher than us.'

Some women had come to the well to fill water; they were talking among themselves.

'As he started with his dinner he gave the order, "go and get some fresh water."'

'It is as if these men feel envious of us when they see us sitting comfortably at home.'

'Yes, they cannot make themselves get up and fetch the water themselves. They will just order, "Go and get the water"—as if we are their maid servants.'

'What are you if not a maid? Don't you get your food? And I'm sure you manage to snatch five or ten rupees also. What else is being a maid?'

'Don't make me feel humiliated sister. I keep craving for even a moment of relaxation. If I were doing so much work at someone else's place I would be living much more comfortably. And on top of it he would feel obliged of me. Here you may give up you life toiling for them but no one would care for you.'

After both of them filled water and gone Gangi came out of the shadow of the tree and came near the platform of the well. The carefree lot too had gone away. Thakur too was heading towards the courtyard of his house to go to sleep after closing his door. Gangi heaved a sigh of relief. After all the field was now clear. Even the prince who had gone to steal the nectar in the days gone by would perhaps not have proceeded so carefully and with so much caution. Gangi climbed the platform with stealthy steps; never earlier had she had a similar experience of victory.

She put the noose of the rope round the neck of the *ghada*. She looked towards her left and right cautiously as if a soldier was going to bore a hole in the castle wall of the enemy in the night. If she is caught now then there will be no hope for her for any pardon or concession. In the end she steeled he heart, remembering her god and lowered the container in the well.

The *ghada* went down and fell in the water very quietly. There was not a sound. Gangi pulled the rope a few snatches and the *ghada* reached almost up to the mouth of the well. Even some brawny wrestler would not have pulled it up so quickly.

Gangi bent down to pick up the container and keep it on the platform when suddenly the door of Thakur *Sahib* opened. Even the face of a lion would not have been more terrifying.

The rope went out of Gangi's hands. Along with the rope the container fell down loudly and for a few moments the sounds of waves could be heard.

'Who is there, who is there?' asked loudly the Thakur as he approached the well. Gangi jumped down from the platform and ran.

When she reached home she found Zokhu was drinking the dirty water putting his mouth to the *lota*.

Captain Saheb

For Zagat Singh going to school was no less unpleasant than having quinine or drinking fish oil. He was a young man who was at heart a wanderer and a drifter. He would sometimes go towards the guava orchards and apart from eating guavas he would savour the foul abuses of the gardeners. Sometime he would take a tour of the rivers and sitting with boatmen in small boats he would cross over to the villages on the other side. He enjoyed being scolded and would not allow any occasion of getting scolded go by. Clapping from behind a horse rider, catching hold of one horse carts from the behind and pulling them towards him, copying the manner of walking of old people were his ways of entertaining himself.

A lazy person does not do any work but he is a slave of his addictions and addictions are not complete without money. Zagat Singh would steal money from home whenever he would find an occasion. If could not find cash he would not hesitate to pick up even utensils or clothes. There were lot of glass vials and bottles at home; he had all of them sent to the second hand goods shops one by one. There were so many things from the old times lying at home: not one of them remained thanks to him. He was so adapt at this art that one marvelled at his dexterity and his mastery over this art. Once he climbed the roof of his two story house from the outside taking the help of the projections and came down carrying a huge metal plate. People at home did not get even a sound of it.

His father *Thakur* Bhakt Singh was the postmaster at the post office of their small town. It was after considerable running around on his part, that his officers had given him the charge of a postmaster in a town. But none of the ideas with which he had come here could be fulfilled. On the other hand it was a net loss that he suffered: back in the villages he used to get all those vegetables, cow dung cakes and fuel free of charge; here they were not available anymore. It was an old habitation he was in where he could not pressurize or trouble anyone. In this state of near adversity, the antics of Zagat Singh really annoyed him. So many times he had thrashed him mercilessly. Zagat Singh would bear the blows silently even though he was quite stout; had he grabbed the hand of his father he would not be able to release it; yet, he was not so defiant. Of course beatings, threats or scolding did not affect him a bit.

The moment Zagat Singh would step into the house there would be a cacophony all around; his mother would go around nagging him, his sisters would start abusing him as if it was some bull that had entered. People at home were averse even to seeing his visage. This kind of contempt exhibited by those at home made him shameless. As for discomforts, he had become almost immune to them. He would lie down wherever when he would feel sleepy, eat whatever he could find.

As the people at home got acquainted with the secrets of his art of stealing they became more and more cautious of him. It came to an end that once for one full month he could not make any headway. The debt of supplier of hashish mounted. The vendor of *ganza* started making angry demands for his arrears. The seller of sweetmeats started talking in bitter tones. It became difficult for poor Zagat to survive. Day and night he would on the prowl but he could never find any occasion. Finally one day his luck turned.

That day, when Bhakt Singh left the post office in the afternoon, he kept a registered envelope in his pocket. 'Who knows some carrier or postman may do some mischief' he thought. However, when he reached home he did not have the presence of mind anymore to take out the letter from the pocket of his coat. Zagat Singh was already on the prey. When he groped the pocket of his father's coat he found an envelope. There were stamps of a number of *annas* on it. He had stolen stamps on a number of occasions and sold them at half the price. He grabbed the envelope immediately—had he known that it had notes inside it he would not have touched it. When he tore open the envelope and notes came out of it he was in a big dilemma. It was as if that torn envelope was admonishing him loudly at the top its voice for his foul deed. His state was like that of a hunter who goes out for shooting birds but ends up shooting a human being instead by mistake. There was repentance, shame and sadness in his heart but he did not have the strength to bear the punishment. He kept the notes in the envelope and went out.

It was summer. Everyone at home was asleep during the afternoon but there was no sleep in the eyes of Zagat. Today he would be getting a real bad deal; there was no doubt of that. It was not right for him to stay at home; better to slip away somewhere for five or ten days. By then the anger of these people would subside. But it would not help unless he goes away somewhere far off otherwise he would not be able to stay unnoticed for long. Someone or the other would give away his whereabouts and he would be caught. But for going away somewhere far off he would need to have some money. Why not he takes out one note from the envelope? They will surely find out that he had torn the envelope; then where is the harm in taking out a note from it. *Dada* has money; he would pay up for it whether he likes it or not. Thinking that he took out a note of ten rupees but at that very instant a new thought came to his mind. It would be great fun if he runs away with all this money and opens a shop in some other town. Then why would he have to steal small amounts every now and then. After some time he would amass a lot of money and then when he comes back people at home would be so surprised.

He took out the envelope once again. There were two hundred rupees in all inside it. With two hundred his shop would be able to run very well. After all what is there in the shop of Murari except for a few big pans and pots to boil milk and a few brass plates. Yet he lives so comfortably and smokes *charas* worth rupees. He puts wagers of ten rupees in one move. If he was not making profit, from where he would meet those expenses? He was so lost in those happy thoughts that his mind went out of his control like someone who loses his foothold in the spate of flood and he is swept away by waves.

That very evening he left for Bombay. Next day a case was filed against Bhakt Singh for embezzlement of money.

II

In the huge parade ground of Bombay fort a band was playing and the handsome young soldiers of the Rajput Regiment were engaged in their regular drill. The way wind makes and breaks the clouds in numerous formations, the leader of the platoon was making the soldiers march in new formations every now and then.

When the maneuvers got over a well built man came and stood in front of the head of the platoon. The captain asked what his name was. The soldier made a salute and said, 'Zagat Singh.'

'What do you want?'

'I want to be admitted in the army.'

'You are not afraid of dying?'

'Not at all. I am a Rajput.'

'You will have to toil really hard.'

'I am not afraid of that.'

'You will also have to go to Aden.'

'I will go gladly,'

The captain noticed that the young man was very quick witted, gallant and full of courage. He was admitted to the forces immediately. The third day the regiment left for Aden. However as the ship moved forwards, the heart of Zagat Singh was getting left behind. As long as the land was visible he kept standing on the deck of the ship watching it fondly. When it could not be seen anymore he took a cold breath and started crying covering his head. Today for the first time he remembered his dear ones. That small town, that hashish shop, all that roaming around, those throngs of loving friends started hovering around in his mind. Who knows if he would ever meet them again? Once he felt so restless that he felt like jumping into the sea.

III

Zagat Singh had been at Aden for three month. All sorts of new things that he encountered there kept him mesmerised for many days but after that old sentiments started reviving again. Now sometimes he would remember his affectionate mother who used to defend him even from the rage of his father and the reproaches of his sister and the contempt of those close to him. He remembered the day when he had fallen sick one day. There was no hope of his survival but neither his father nor his sisters were concerned about it. It was only his mother who would stay by his bedside the entire night and provide comfort in his pains by her sweet and affectionate words. Those days he had seen that goddess-like figure crying during the night. She was herself getting worn out by diseases but looking after him she had forgotten her own plight as if she had no discomfort whatsoever.

Would he ever be able to see his mother again? Feeling regretful and disappointed in this manner he would sometimes go to the seashore and watch for hours the immense and endless flow of water. Since many days he had been getting a desire to send a letter but due to shame and remorse he had been putting it off. Finally one day when he could not bear it anymore he wrote a letter asking for forgiveness for his misdeeds. The letter was full of reverence from the beginning to the end and in the end he gave an assurance to his mother; 'Dear mother I have been doing enormous amount of mischief and you people had got sick of me. I feel truly ashamed for all those mistakes and I promise to you that if I remain alive I will do something or the other to prove myself. Then perhaps you will not have any hesitation in calling me your son. Please give your blessings so that I am able to fulfill my pledge.'

After finishing the letter he dropped it in the letterbox and started waiting for a reply from that day itself; however a month passed without a reply. Now he started feeling restless—I hope mother is not ill. *Dada* perhaps did not write out of anger. I hope some other calamity has not befallen on them. Under a tree in the camp some soldiers had installed a statue of black stone. Some worshipful soldiers used to make offering of water to that statue every day. Zagat Singh used to make fun of them; but now like a person who had lost his senses he kept sitting before that statue with his eyes closed. He was sitting in that meditative posture when someone called him by his name. That was an orderly from the office who had brought a letter for him. When Zagat Singh held the letter in his hand his entire body trembled. Taking the name of the God he opened the letter and read. It was written: 'Your father has been sentenced for five year of imprisonment on charges of embezzlement. Your mother is almost on her deathbed due to this grief. Come home if you can get leave.'

Zagat Singh went immediately to the Captain and said, 'Sir my mother is ill, please allow me to take some leave.'

The Captain looked at him sternly and said, 'leave cannot be allowed right now.'

'Then you please accept my resignation'

'Resignation too cannot be accepted now.'

'I can't stay here even for an instant.'

'You will have to stay. You people have to go to war very soon.'

'The war has begun! Oh, then I won't be able to go home? When are we going to leave?'

'Very soon… in two to four days.'

IV

Four years have passed by. There is no fighter like Captain Zagat Singh in that regiment. In face of difficult circumstances his valour gets even more excited. In any mission where everyone else gives up it is he whose task it is to fulfil it. He is forever ahead of everyone when it comes to an attack; there is never a crease on his forehead. On top of that he is so humble, so solemn but still so good-humoured that all the officers as well subordinates are full of praise for him. He seems to have got transformed. His officers have so much faith on him that they consult him on everything. Whoever it may be he would give a long list of his exploits: how he set fire to the German magazine, how he rescued his captain from the barrage of machine guns, how he managed to come back carrying an injured soldier on his shoulders. It seems he has no attachment for his life, as if he is searching for his end! During the night however when Zagat Singh finds some leisure, sitting all alone in his tent he remembers the people at home and then a few drops of tears would come out of his eyes. Every month he sends home a big part of his salary and not one week would go by when he would not write a letter to his mother. He is worried the most for his father who is suffering the torture of prison due to his misdeeds. When would the day come when he would place his head on his feet and ask forgiveness for his offence and he would bless him putting his hand on his head?

V

Four and a quarter years have gone by. It is evening. There is a big crowd in front of the Naini Jail. So many convicts have finished their term in the prison that day. Their relatives have come to take them back but the old Bhakt Singh is sitting in his cell feeling sad. His back has become bent like a bow. His body is reduced to a skeleton. He looks like a statue of some victim of famine that has been made by an expert sculptor. His term too has come to an end today; however no one from his family is there. Who would come? Who remained there who could come? An old but well built prisoner came and shook his shoulder—so Bhakt, has any one come from your home?

'Who is there at home?' he said in a trembling voice.

'You will go home at least?'

'Where is my home?'

'So you will keep staying here?'

'If they don't throw me out, then I would stay on.'

Today after four years Bhakt Singh was remembering his ill treated and exiled son because of whom his life had got ruined, his reputation reduced to dirt and his family shattered. Even his memory was unbearable; however today sinking in the immense sea of hopelessness and sorrow he clutched to that straw itself; god knows what state he is in. He may be a rouge but after all he is his son, the symbol of the family. When I die he would at least shed some tear; he would at least make an offering of a palm-full of water! I never treated him with love and affection. Whenever he did any mischief I would pounce on him. Once when he entered the kitchen without washing his feet I had hung him upside down as a punishment. How many times I had slapped him for talking loudly. Even though I had got the gift of a son I did not respect it; today I am suffering the punishment for that. Where the bond of affection is so weak how such family can be saved?

VI

The morning had broken. The sun of hope came out. How pleasant and mellow were its rays today, how pure the air, how beautiful the sky, how green the trees and how sweet sounding the chorus of the birds. The entire nature was painted in the colours of hope; however for Bhakt Singh it was darkness all around.

The officer in charge of the prison arrived. The prisoners were sitting in a row. The officer was calling the names of the prisoners one by one and gave them the order of their release. The faces of the prisoners were full of hope. Whoever was called would go happily to the officer, receive the order, salute him with a bow and after embracing the others who were his companions during the time of his adversity go out. His family members would come running and embrace him. Someone was showering handful of coins, others distributing sweets and elsewhere the employees of the prison were being given a reward.

In the end the name of Bhakt Singh was called. He went to the jailer walking very slowly with his head bent downwards and with a sad face took the order and walked towards the prison gate as if he was approaching a rough sea. Coming out of the gate he sat down on the ground wondering where to do now?

Suddenly he noticed an army officer on horseback approaching the prison. He was wearing a khaki uniform and an embroidered turban. He was sitting on the horse with a strange kind of dignity. Behind him followed a phaeton. Noticing the officer the prison guards held their guns in arm and standing in a single file gave him a salute.

Bhakt Singh said to himself, 'There is some lucky fellow for whom a phaeton has come to receive him and here is one unfortunate wretch for whom there is not even a place to go.'

The army officer looked here and there and then dismounting from the horse he came and stood in front of Bhakt Singh. Bhakt Singh looked at him carefully and then got up with a surprise and said, 'Oh Zagat Singh, my son!'

Zagat Singh fell to his feet crying.

#

Thank you for reading this book. If you enjoyed it won't you please take a moment to leave a review at Amazon.com. Even a few lines or words of yours will provide great satisfaction to the author.

Dinesh Verma

Glossary

1. Kalabattu: also called *Zardozi* or *Zari*, kalabattu is a form of embroidery in which gold and silver threads are used on silk, brocade or velvet fabric.
2. *Chikan*: another kind of traditional Indian embroidery in which thread (most often white, though other colours too are sometimes used) is used on white muslin, fine cotton or voile fabric to make motifs of flowers and animals.
3. *Chausar*: also known as *Chaupar*, is an indigenous board game played in India.
4. *Ganjifa*: also known as *Ganjapha* is an indigenous card game played in some parts of India.
5. *Paan*: a preparation made with betel leaf, areca nut, *katha* paste and slaked lime, which is chewed after a meal in India.
6. *Bigadu*: one who tends to spoil any work that he may be assigned.
7. *Ji*: a common suffix in Hindi and Urdu, used with proper names or titles as a mark of added respect.
8. *Yaar*: means a friend in Hindi and Urdu.
9. *Wali*: a holy man.
10. English Company: The East India Company, which started as a British company for trading in India but later took over the control of a vast area of the country and was thus the founder of the British colonial rule in India. The colonial adminstration was formally taken over by the British Crown from the East India Company in 1858.
11. The Resident: An officer appointed in each Princely state to liaise between the colonial administration and the King or the Prince of the state concerned in India.
12. Nawab Asafudollah: Asaf-ud-Daula was appointed as the nawab wazir of Awadh in 1775. Lucknow was the capital of the Awadh state.
13. *Chillum*: a small clay pipe used for smoking tobacco.

14. *Janab*: a Persian word which means 'your Excellency' or 'your honour'.
15. *Ahinsa*: means non violence in Hindi.
16. Department of Salt: The taxation on salt was introduced by the East India Company in 1835 and was a major source of revenue.
17. *Pir*: a title for a *Sufi* master a saint or spiritual guide. After the death of a *Pir* his grave and tomb become objects of reverence and periodic worship.
18. *Chaddar*: the sheet which covers the grave of a *Pir* on which the devotees make their offerings.
19. *Munshiji*: a respected title used during the British days for a man who would acquire learning. It was also used for addressing secretaries, clerks and accountants.
20. *Babuji*: from *babu* used in Indian sub-continent as a term of respect towards men. With the honorific suffix *ji* added to it, *babuji* is a word used to address one's father or a respected elder.
21. *Gulli-danda*: also known as *gilli-danda*, it is a sport played in small town and rural areas in Indian sub-continent. *gulli-danda* is played with two sticks: a large one called a *danda* which is used to hit the smaller one which is called *gulli*.
22. *Dada*: a term used for father.
23. *Kabbadi*: an indigenous sport in Indian sub-continent which is played between two competing teams in which a member of one team goes to the court of the other with an object of touching any one of them and coming back safely, which is all to be done taking only a single breath. If he is caught and not allowed to come back without losing his breath the opposing team wins a point. It is now a well recognised sport played even in major sport meets like Asian Games.
24. *Dal, roti*: *dal* is a slightly thick soup prepared with lentils, peas or beans which is eaten with roti or *chappati*, which in turn is a *gallete* or flat bread made from unleavened wheat flour dough.
25. *Panch, panchayat, panch parmeshwar*: A *panchayat* is an assembly of five elders or respected persons of the village nominated for the resolution of a given dispute. In Hindi, *panchayat* literally means an *ayat* or assembly of *panch* of five persons. A *panchyat* has been a well-recognized institution for

dispute resolution in the Indian villages for centuries. A *Panch* is one of the five elders selected. *Parmeshwar* means the supreme divine power or God. It is a general saying that the decision of the *Panchas* is like the decision given by the supreme being as the *panchas* are expected to be absolutely unbiased and objective.

26. *Guruji*: guru in Hindi means a teacher.
27. *Bigha*: is a unit of measurement of land. One bigha is equivalent to about 1600 square yards.
28. *Mian*: a title of respect like 'sir' in Urdu. In the present context the respect is mixed with some element of endearment as it is used between two persons who are almost equal in standing.
29. Digging out my roots, or *jad khodna* is a Hindi proverb which means doing something that causes some serious harm to someone.
30. 'He has separated the milk from the water.....' *Dudh ka dudh aur pani ka pani*. A Hindi proverb which means 'giving a very clear and objective decision in a given matter'.
31. *Bania*: a person from the *vaishya* caste usually engaged in commerce or trade.
32. *Thakur*: a person from the *Kashtriya* caste. A term generally used for people from Rajput caste in Uttar Pradesh and Bihar.
33. *Puri*: round flat bread smaller than roti which is cooked by deep frying in heated oil.
34. *Chutni*: a condiment made of herbs and spices which serves as an accompaniment to various types of food items in Indian cuisine.
35. *Raita*: a slightly thick soup made of yogurt in which finely chopped cucumber, onion or tomatoes are sometimes mixed.
36. *Mithai*: a sweetmeat or traditional Indian confectionary item.
37. *Pattal*: a plate made by attaching together a number of big leaves.
38. *Anna*: a denomination of money used prior to introduction of currency in vogue now. Four *annas* equaled one rupee.
39. *Seer*: a measure of weight used in India before introduction of metric system. A *seer* was equal to 1.25 kg
40. Vaikunth: the abode of god Vishnu in Hindu mythology.

41. *Dhoti*: a garment which covers the lower body.
42. *Kurta*: a shirt which reaches up to the knees and with long sleeves.
43. *Babuji*: here it means father.
44. *Khaddar*: a coarse cotton homespun cloth.
45. *Lutiya*: derivative from *lota*. A *lota* is a round shaped metallic container little taller than a glass to fill water. A *lutiya* is a smaller version of a *lota*.
46. *Bahuji, bhaiya: Bahuji* is a respectful term to address the lady of the house. *Bhaiya* means brother.
47. *Tulsi*: basil plant which is considered as holy by Hindus.
48. *Sindur*: vermillion power put in the parting of the hair by Indian women. It signifies the married status of a woman.
49. *Barat*: a marriage procession.
50. *Ghee*: refined butter.
51. *Thakurain*: wife of a *Thakur*.
52. *Pargana*: an erstwhile administrative unit in the Indian sub-continent.
53. Pous and Magh: two winter months in Indian calendar that roughly corresponds to December and January.
54. *Halku*: In colloquial Hindi it means one who is very light.
55. *Nilgai*: A blue bull or a blue cow, *nilgai* is an antelope found in the Indian sub-continent.
56. *Lota*: see *lutiya* at 45 above.
57. "Is it because they wear a thread around their neck?" A reference to the sacred thread that a person of higher caste especially Brahmins used to wear as a mark of their initiation.
58. "it is as if their maternal grandmother is going to die": from a Hindi proverb, '*nani marna*', which literally means the death of the maternal grandmother. As most children in traditional Indian set up used to be very close to their maternal grandmother, her death would indeed be a grievous loss to them.
59. *Ghada*: a round earthen pot used to fill and store water.

About the translator

Dinesh Verma studied English Literature in the University of Delhi before joining the Indian Revenue Service. He is an alumnus of Hindu College, Delhi and also of Institut International d'Administrations Publique and the Ecole Nationale des Ponts et Chaussées, Paris. He has also attended courses at Syracuse University, New York and at Harvard Business School. Presently he is based at Delhi.

Dinesh Verma is the author of a collection of stories, *'The Fine Print and Other Yarns'*, which was published by UBS Publishers Pvt Ltd., New Delhi in 2009. It is now being distributed in the digital form at Amazon.Com and in hard-copy format by Createspace.

Dinesh Verma is presently working on his first novel, 'The Parisian Interlude.'

To find out more about the author go to: www.dineshvermadelhi.com

Other works by Dinesh Verma

The Fine Print and other Yarns

The Fine Print and other Yarns was the first book written by Dinesh Verma. It is a collection of nine stories some of which may well be classified as novella as they run into thirty to fifty pages.

The first four stories are set in Paris of 1980s and the next three in Paris of 1990s. The last two are set in India around the turn of the last century.

Even though each story in this collection presents a different character who has nothing in common with the others, all of them have one theme in common: the travails of an expatriate or a migrant in a foreign land. Each story deals with someone who is trying to come to terms with his circumstances in a place different from the place of his origin. They explore thus the spirit of enterprise, freedom and tenacity that is the hallmark of an expatriate. [Read the brief write up by Dinesh Verma: 'A tribute to the spirit of enterprise, freedom and tenacity of humankind']

The collection is, therefore, like a kaleidoscope, each turn of which presents an eminently interesting and unforgettable character. Among them are:

Buddy, a young lecturer in Delhi University in 1980s, who has a strange fascination for the bohemian life of painters in Paris but whose exposure to them is limited to what he has read in Moon and Sixpence and Lust for Life. Buddy, who has been dreaming all his life of visiting Paris, gets a rare opportunity, though for just two days for what he thinks would be a rare opportunity to experience firsthand the life of painters and artists in Paris.

However, what Buddy comes across in Paris of 1980s does not quite correspond to the image of life of Impressionist painters that he has been carrying in his mind and what follows is like an exorcism for him.

Krishnan, who has an ambition to become a marketing guru and who is doing his MBA from a reputed Business School in Paris, is invited for dinner to an elegant high-end restaurant in a chic quartier of Paris by a colleague on her birthday. The dinner in that posh restaurant proves to be a lesson in marketing skills for Krishnan, though one that he has to learn the hard way.

Dr Chopra, a widely traveled Indian doctor who considers himself to be the last word on foreign travel is on his first visit to the city of fashion and romance. Not knowing a word of French, the jet setting doctor finds himself driven to the point of utter hopelessness and despair finding his way to his hotel from the airport. Not able to carry out even basic communication with anyone, he feels like a child who has been separated from parents in a big fair and thinks of taking a flight back to Delhi the same day. Yet in two days he starts liking Paris so much that he is already planning his next trip there.

Pieter Van Der Polder, a Dutch young man who cooks his dinner with a finesse and attention to details that would remind one of a classical music performer, gets into a really interesting battle of wits with a Belgian girl on his floor.

Amitabh, a young man who is in Paris for a year with merely five hundred dollars that the foreign exchange rules allow him to carry out of India and a meager living allowance, finds his long standing reputation of being a generous and hospitable person getting evaporated into thin air. He undergoes such a transformation within a few days of his arrival in Paris that he would put to shame a confirmed miser.

A young mobile phone dealer in Delhi, who became multimillionaire almost overnight selling mobile phones, soon after the introduction of mobile telephony in Indian markets and then reduced to penury due to a sudden reversal of his fortunes, is once again on an upward trajectory in his business. Travelling from New Delhi to Chennai by train, he relates in a very brash and candid manner the tale of his shady business deals to his fellow passengers, not knowing that there is a dangerous person amongst his audience.

Bawa, a corporate executive in New Delhi buys a new Indian car in late 1980s, which is based on the technology of 1950s. He is in love with his new car. However, once he moves to Mumbai for a new assignment, he finds his beloved car getting transformed into virtually an antique after the influx of a host of new generation Japanese and German cars in the Indian market in early 1990s.

Apart from the interesting characters and situations, these stories portray the lives of a cross section of Indians finding their way out in a foreign society; quite unlike the one they had been used to before leaving India. These stories provide a rare insight into the psyche of an average Indian and his resilience and adaptability, which are the hallmark of the Indian diaspora.

The Fine Print and other Yarns is available as an e-Book at Amazon.com and other online retailers. Hard copy of the book is available at Createspace.com.

Printed in Great Britain
by Amazon